W9-BZC-963

Tired of waiting for Miranda to remove her jeans, Taylor unzipped them and ripped them off herself before pushing Miranda's hand back into place.

Taking the hint, Miranda pressed firmly and let Taylor guide her hand in a quick, side-to-side motion. Miranda continued faster and harder as Taylor's body tensed approvingly in response.

"That's it, baby," Taylor groaned from deep within her throat.

About the Author

Tracey Richardson, who was born in Windsor, Ontario, has worked as a reporter for newspapers in southwestern Ontario and is currently a copy editor at a daily newspaper. She and her partner live in cottage country in Ontario's Georgian Bay area with their Labrador retriever Cleo. When not sitting before a computer, Tracey enjoys motorcycling, golfing, hiking, skating, skiing, and just about any sport.

NORTHERN BLUE

TRACEY RICHARDSON

THE NAIAD PRESS, INC.
1996

Copyright © 1996 by Tracey Richardson

All rights reserved. No part of this book may be reproduced or transmitted in any form or by any means, electronic or mechanical, including photocopying, without permission in writing from the publisher.

Printed in the United States of America on acid-free paper
First Edition

Editor: Lisa Epson
Cover designer: Bonnie Liss (Phoenix Graphics)
Typesetter: Sandi Stancil

Library of Congress Cataloging-in-Publication Data

Richardson, Tracey, 1964 –
   Northern blue / Tracey Richardson.
      p.   cm.
   ISBN 1-56280-118-X
   1. Lesbians—Canada—Fiction.   I. Title.
PS3568.I3195N67   1996
813'.54—dc20   95-39246
                                                                      CIP

For Sandra,
my very own hero in blue

Acknowledgments

My foremost thanks to my good friend Dorothea, who has always encouraged me to write a novel and was instrumental in getting me off my butt to actually do it. She also deserves my gratitude for carefully reading numerous drafts and making suggestions. My loving thanks to my partner, Sandra Green for giving me her expertise and support and for providing the home for my heart. Thanks to Beth for cheering me on. My gratitude to Naiad, for giving a first-time author a break.

CHAPTER ONE

The piercing buzz of the alarm clock planted a tiny, irritating seed of consciousness in Miranda McCauley's exhausted slumber.

She was back in school. High school. The bell was shrilling its warning that class was about to begin. But where was that damned classroom anyway? Panicked, Miranda began running up the empty hall. Lost and confused, she jogged through the labyrinth of corridors, her head throbbing with the bell.

Now the bell was smashing into her dream, fragmenting her visions, sending her from school

1

hallways to noisy traffic jams to a hockey arena. At last, she could no longer hold onto any vision, wakefulness coming abruptly.

Jesus, where am I? Blindly, she reached over and smacked the alarm clock off with her fist.

Shit! I gotta get up, she thought wearily as she forced herself to sit up, remembering she was in her cement-block dorm room at the Ontario Police College. Her roommate, Cheryl (or cellmate as the young recruits liked to joke of the dorms), still snored away in oblivion.

Miranda pushed herself from the tiny bed that felt cramped to her five-foot-eight athletic frame. It definitely wasn't the cushiony, queen-sized bed from home.

At least today, the third day of classes in the twelve-week recruit training program, was a PFA day (Physical Fitness Activity, or Push your Fucking Ass, as it was better known), Miranda remembered hopefully.

She slipped into the shower just in time before the mad scramble of women recruits, glad Cheryl was a couple of minutes behind her. She looked forward to the unfolding day. She loved sports and physical training; it came easy to her, the way math did to some, or fixing cars to others. In high school, she had been a countywide track star and one of the best female basketball players in the province. She went on to excel at university sports, too, playing varsity basketball and helping her team win a championship.

Not surprisingly, her fitness test at the college on the first day had been a mere cakewalk. In fact, the sergeant in charge of the fitness program told her she had finished among the top three of all the forty-nine female recruits. But that's no excuse not to keep busting your butt, he had scowled at her.

In the cafeteria, Miranda sat with two other female recruits, gulping down a bowl of cold, mushy Cream of Wheat. She had already discovered it was best to grab something quick and easy from the serving tables. It made for less time to endure the lecherous stares and the snide, whispered (and sometimes not-so-whispered) remarks from her male counterparts in line. They outnumbered the women by about three to one and took a certain macho pride in relegating the women to sexual terms.

"She's got a nice ass," one would comment just audible enough for the woman to hear.

"Yeah, but her tits aren't big enough," was a common retort.

This morning, the three classmates sat huddled in T-shirts, track pants, and running shoes. Usually, the complex saw a multitude of police uniforms with cadets expected to wear the uniform of the department that had hired them. Fitness and sports offered the only aberration from the dress code.

"Jesus, I'm so nervous, I can't even eat," ranted Vicki Mason, a young cadet from Toronto.

"What for?" Miranda's eyebrows shot up.

" 'Cause of Whiteside, that's what for. Everybody says she's a real bitch. Likes to pick somebody and make chopped liver out of them in front of the class!" Vicki could visualize herself being thrown to the mat and made a fool of in the upcoming

3

self-defense class, and she didn't like it one bit, her face souring at the thought of it.

In disgust, she threw her half-eaten piece of toast onto her plate. "I just know it'll be me — I can feel it!"

Taylor Whiteside's reputation was well known to recruits before they even arrived at the academy. Graduates would go back to their departments spewing venom about the academy's martial arts and self-defense instructor. She was tough, they'd said, and it wasn't below her to humiliate the cadets to keep them in their place.

"Aw c'mon, Vic. How much of a monster can she be," Miranda sneered. "Police departments want their graduates back in one piece."

"Hey, you guys, we won't be in one piece for long if we're not out on the track in five minutes," Miranda's roommate Cheryl Johnson warned. "Let's go."

After twenty minutes of calisthenics and a twenty-minute jog, the twenty-six members of C-Class moved on to the dreaded two-hour self-defense class. The spring class of 1991 was actually divided up into four classes of cadets who came from police forces across Ontario. Here these men and women would become trained and certified constables. They would be ready to carry guns and patrol the streets.

The class formed at the front of the gymnasium, the recruits chatting nervously among themselves. Striding into the room, her eyes devoid of emotion, Sgt. Taylor Whiteside barked, "CLASS!"

She smiled to herself at the recruits nervously snapping to attention. *But not quite fast enough,* she mentally noted.

The veteran instructor confidently took her place at the front of the class and stood, hands behind her back, staring down each recruit, etching their faces into her memory. She paused, letting their barely-concealed agitation — and what she hoped was fear — build. She was well aware of the reputation she'd worked hard to attain. To her, a little bit of fear went a long way to keep them in line.

Taylor Whiteside was a big woman. She stood an inch short of six feet and was built like a tree trunk. Her wrists and legs were thick like a man's — prime evidence of her growing up on a Saskatchewan farm. On the fringe of her fortieth birthday, her short dark hair was richly flecked with silver and was graying at the temples. Her face was strong and handsome, but most striking about her were her piercing, steel-blue eyes. One minute they could shoot daggers, the next they could ooze charm.

But charm was the last thing the recruits were about to see. Whiteside narrowed her eyes as she appraised the new class, her well-practiced act flawless by now. Slowly walking down the column length of recruits, she looked at each one, defying them to dare eye contact.

"So you think you've got what it takes to be a good cop," she said acidly to no one in particular. "You think you can handle what the street can throw at you." It wasn't a question.

A dropped pin could have been heard as everyone collectively sucked in their breath, waiting for the next moment.

Whiteside's pace increased, up and down the column. "Maybe it's time for you to show me." Stopping in front of a beefy young man, she poked her index finger into his chest. "You — front and center."

As he stepped forward, Whiteside walked to a nearby cabinet and removed a steel black tonfa stick, a standard piece of police equipment that had replaced the old nightstick. Its visible difference was a handle on the side of it, allowing its owner a sturdier grasp.

Smiling, she handed the tonfa to the rookie. "Take my head off with this — c'mon!"

The recruit looked dubiously at the tonfa, then at Whiteside. He gripped the side handle and made a tentative swing at the instructor's head. Dissatisfied, Whiteside stepped back. "Like your life depends on it, you useless piece of shit!"

The man clamped his jaw and swung the tonfa at Whiteside's head. She smartly sidestepped and gripped the recruit's right forearm with her right hand. With her left, she chopped hard on his elbow, sending the stick careening through the air. He grunted in surprise as she slowly forced him to the ground, his arm twisted behind his back.

Whiteside surveyed the group for her next victim. A few were working their mouths, trying to mask a giggle or a contemptuous grin.

"You," she directed to Vicki Mason, who had been trying her damnedest not to make any face at all. "Up here."

Vicki stole a quick glance in the direction of her neighbors in a futile hope that it wasn't her that Whiteside wanted. Vicki was nearly as big as her instructor, but her demeanor wasn't so tough. In fact, she could be quite easily cowed.

Miranda watched her friend step forward and was

surprised at the envy pricking her. She wasn't sure why she wanted to be up there — it wasn't as though she felt she could knock her instructor down a peg or two, or that she wanted to show off. She just knew she'd like to see firsthand how good Whiteside was, how strong she was. Could she really be that hard-nosed or was it a facade? Miranda was intrigued.

Miranda studied Whiteside as she planted herself behind Vicki, crooking an arm around her neck. Deftly, she squeezed Vicki in a steel-like vise, simultaneously pulling her backward and off balance. In seconds, Vicki's dark skin began to pale as she gasped for air.

A couple recruits stirred and whispered, wondering why Whiteside wasn't letting her go. They felt helpless, too intimidated to say anything as Vicki tipped on the brink of unconsciousness. Finally, Whiteside relaxed her grip and gently ushered the limp Vicki to a sitting position on the mat.

Miranda was impressed. Tuning out Whiteside's explanation of the carotid restraint, Miranda studied her broad shoulders, massive arms, and thick legs. Her obvious strength wowed Miranda.

"What's your name and PD?"

"Vicki Mason," the young recruit rasped. "Metro Toronto."

"Okay, Mason, now you know how it's done." Without hesitation, Whiteside lifted Vicki's elbow and prodded her back to her spot. "Now I'm going to show you these two moves in slow motion, and you're going to spend the next hour practicing on each other. Got it? Okay, another volunteer front and center!"

Miranda swallowed and stepped out. Sweat rolled down her sides in tiny droplets as she stood before Whiteside, anticipating what was to come. She liked to confront things that scared her. Get it over with, she always told herself, knowing the unknown was the scariest of all.

She told herself to breathe. Relax. Be cool.

"Miranda McCauley, Hooperstown PD," she boldly proclaimed before being asked.

A hint of a smile creased Whiteside's lips. Quick learner or a smart-ass? She'd soon find out.

Jumping behind Miranda, she clamped a thick arm around her neck.

"The key is to be quick. Take them by surprise. Get behind like this, plant yourself, bend your elbow, and squeeze hard."

With that, Whiteside's forearm clamped tighter. "Now try to get loose," she commanded, her face just inches from Miranda's flushed cheek.

Miranda squirmed, then tried to pry Whiteside's arm loose. But it only prompted the instructor to grab Miranda's left arm with her free arm and twist it behind her back. Miranda was only three inches shorter than the hulking woman behind her, but the twenty-four-year-old's lean athletic build left her easily outweighed by thirty-five pounds or more.

It was useless. She couldn't budge her no matter what. And with each attempt, Whiteside only squeezed harder.

"Now you're trying to get them off balance too. Pull them back into your body."

Whiteside finally released Miranda, who turned her reddened face to her. "Can I try?" she panted, trying not to sound too eager or too confident. She knew the game.

Whiteside crossed her arms before her thick chest. Her eyebrows shot up in surprise before settling over darkening blue eyes. Whatever this kid's motives were, they'd be shot down in a hell of a hurry. "Sure. Get behind me."

Miranda pressed herself against Whiteside's strong, broad back. She felt thick and hard. Her neck was wide too, but her hair seemed so soft, almost baby fine. It seemed such a paradox, such soft hair on someone so tough, so hard. Miranda felt herself wanting to touch it — to run her fingertips through it, to feel its softness intertwining with her skin.

She forced the thoughts from her head, feeling Whiteside's impatience. Planting her arm around her instructor's neck, she quickly pulled Whiteside's weight into her own and, with her elbow crooked, clamped down on her neck.

"C'mon, harder," Whiteside gasped. "That's it."

Miranda released her grip, pleased with herself. She hoped Whiteside was, too.

The instructor turned to Miranda, cynically scanning her face for signs of the usual youthful arrogance all too common in the first week of classes. But there was none. The kid seemed almost shy, but deadly serious. Whiteside was a little disappointed.

"Good work, McCauley," she uttered without looking at the young woman. "Who's next?"

A faint whiff of sweat and the sound of metal

clanging against metal greeted Miranda as she entered the crowded weight room, a towel slung over her shoulder.

Absentmindedly, she climbed on a stationary bicycle and punched the buttons, thoughts of her self-defense class — her second class in as many days — pushing everything else aside. They were welcome thoughts that promised to rescue her from the monotonous pedaling.

She was doing well, she was sure. Her athleticism was paying off in spades, and more than that. She was keen to learn. She was sure Whiteside — ah yes, Taylor Whiteside. Miranda's smile spread along with the warm, tingling sensation in her thighs.

She took a deep breath, not altogether happy with the sensation overtaking her, but not wishing it to go away either. What was it about this woman that made her feel like a love-struck teenager?

For two days now, Miranda had found herself constantly daydreaming of her instructor. What kind of woman was she? Was she really that tough, or was she a marshmallow inside? God, she was sexy — strong and handsome. Such firm hands. But had she even really noticed Miranda?

She closed her eyes, feeling heady. Her breath came hard now, sweat dripping down her face. And it wasn't just from the cycling.

Across the room, Taylor Whiteside exhaled as she pushed the heavy barbell up, feeling the burn in her biceps and pecs. The bar made a clunk as she set it down on the metal rack above her.

From the vinyl bench she stared up at the dirty ceiling tiles. She smiled knowingly. *It's time to find*

some eager little cadet for a little afterschool tutoring.
But who?

Swiftly she sat up and wiped the sweat from her
brow. She couldn't contain a wicked smile. Stretching
her arms above her, she cast hungry eyes about.
Squinting toward the stationary bikes across the
room, she noticed one of her students pedaling
furiously.

Hmmm, McCauley, C-Class. What was her first
name again? Miranda. Miranda McCauley from
Hooperstown, that's it.

She stared long and hard at Miranda across the
room. She'd never really looked at her before. She
was just another faceless, fresh recruit — they all
blended together the first week. But this McCauley,
she was pretty attentive, didn't seem to think she
knew it all like most, Taylor recalled of the two
classes she'd taught her.

Miranda pedaled as if she were on some kind of
suicide mission — either that or she really had
something on her mind, Taylor thought, drinking her
in. The tight, finely-chiseled muscles in her legs
bulged with each turn of the pedal. She certainly
looked the athletic type — wide shoulders, defined
muscles. A pleasant, strong face and an easy smile.
And those deep green eyes, Taylor suddenly
remembered, mentally comparing them to cool brook
water drenched in sunlight. It wasn't that her eyes
needed any more attention, but her high cheekbones
accentuated them even more. Taylor'd never seen
anyone with such captivating eyes.

Miranda hopped off the bike and headed for the
hall where the drinking fountain was, absently

brushing her hand through her short, light brown hair.

Yes, a drink of water would go down good about now, Taylor smiled as she headed for the hall too. She wanted another look at those eyes.

Miranda, her head buried in porcelain, at first didn't notice the woman leaning against the wall beside her, silently watching. A warm shiver tickled her spine.

"Oh, ah, hello, Sergeant Whiteside," Miranda sputtered in surprise, sweat gushing down her face in steady streams. She could feel her face flush a deeper shade as though Taylor could read her mind.

"McCauley," Taylor nodded casually. *God, those eyes!* How could she not have noticed them before? Pools you could dive right into! Taylor, speechless, studied Miranda. She had to restrain herself from commenting on her eyes. Hell, that wouldn't be very cool. *Gotta keep control here.* She straightened herself.

Miranda toweled off her face again, not wanting to move on.

"You look like you're on a real mission, McCauley," Taylor said, her voice back, her eyes moving down Miranda's soaked tank top. They lingered there longer than they should have.

"So do you." Miranda smiled and pointed to Taylor's soaked towel. Her gray T-shirt, with the large block letters **RCMP** stamped across the chest, was damp too.

"Yeah, well, gotta keep up with you young folks," Taylor winked.

So she is human after all, Miranda thought with relief. That familiar warm sensation crept between her legs again.

12

"Keep up the good work, McCauley," Taylor said before disappearing down the hall. She whistled to herself, a new spring in her step.

CHAPTER TWO

Miranda tossed and turned in her cot, each night a carbon copy of the one before. Every time she shut her eyes, images of Taylor Whiteside abducted her mind. Taylor laughing. Taylor smiling. Taylor carefully watching her practice her self-defense maneuvers. Taylor stern-faced, looking her over. Taylor lying next to her. Taylor slowly undressing her . . .

Oh God! Miranda sat bolt upright in bed, drenched in sweat, heart pumping fear through her.

Miranda had never made love with a woman

14

before. At the university she'd had a couple of brief sexual encounters with men, but they hadn't interested her for the most part. There was something warm and reluctantly comfortable about women, and though she pushed those thoughts away, there was something magnetic about them, like the pulling of an invisible undertow. The idea of dating women once briefly intrigued Miranda, until that point guard on her university basketball team — Janet — drunk one night after a big game, had come on to her in Miranda's dorm room, fumbling in an alcoholic haze before passing out.

They never talked about it, and if they had, they would have blamed it on the booze. Since then, Miranda had shunned the idea of making it with a woman. She didn't want any part of it if it were like that. But thoughts of Taylor Whiteside weren't so easy to smother, and she found herself not wanting to.

Miranda propped her hands behind her head, twisting cotton between toes. The more she turned it over in her mind, the more she had to admit the strongest or most important relationships she'd ever formed in her life were with women. Her mother, her grandmother, her dearest friendships, her most intense young crushes.

Was that all Taylor was too — a simple crush? Maybe that had been her big mistake, Miranda thought, fumbling in the dark with another university freshman. Maybe what she'd really needed all along was an older woman, an experienced woman.

She settled back into her cot again, wishing she had the privacy of her own room. She slid her hand down between her legs.

* * * * *

Miranda spent her first Saturday at the police college by herself, submerged in the giddiness of her crush on Taylor Whiteside. Most of the other recruits had taken off for the weekend, but she had rebuffed all invitations. She just couldn't concentrate on anything else.

After eating supper alone, Miranda felt the urge for a couple of solitary brews. Maybe that would dull the anxiety, make her forget about Taylor Whiteside, at least for a little while, until Monday rolled around and she could see her around campus again.

Pulling a white nylon windbreaker over her black turtleneck sweater, Miranda jogged to the bus stop in the damp May air. She'd heard about a quiet little tavern outside of town, the kind that played country music and was a second home to the local yokels. Yeah, that's what she needed. Nobody would know her there. She could sit with her beer totally absorbed in her own thoughts.

Miranda squinted as her eyes adjusted to the darkened, smoky interior. It was just the sort of place she'd expected. A handful of men wearing the local uniform of flannel shirts and ball caps sat at the bar flirting with the buxom barmaid. Miranda paid scant attention to them and parked herself in an empty corner booth.

"What're ya havin'?" the woman drawled. Startled, Miranda looked up into the gum-chewing face of the middle-aged barmaid.

"Just a draft."

Miranda anxiously tapped her fingers on the

chipped table, wishing away thoughts of Taylor Whiteside. If only it were that easy.

Miranda had always found strong, authoritative, older women attractive. Not because she wanted to be dominated, but because she saw them as more confident, developed, and charismatic copies of herself. They were what she hoped to become. But it was more than that with Taylor. Miranda was sure there was a certain vulnerability below the callous layer, and she wanted to mine it.

Hank Williams's "Can't Get You Off My Mind" boomed from the aging jukebox, prompting a groan from Miranda. Why that song? It would have made her laugh were she less introspective.

A large glass of beer thumped down on her table. "Will ya be havin' more later, honey?" the barmaid asked, a little more friendly this time.

"Yeah, sure." Miranda handed her two dollars and took a slow swallow.

Damn! There had to be some way to get Taylor Whiteside's attention. Running into her in the gym was a good start. But that heady little moment was fading quickly. Like a junkie hooked on some elusive drug, Miranda needed another intoxicating fix of the object of her flourishing desire.

Half a beer later, Miranda wandered over to the jukebox. She smiled at the sight of the different titles — all hurting songs from old country stars. Most of them had been recorded long before she was even born. She dropped a quarter into the slot and watched as the arm dropped a 45 onto the turntable.

Taylor Whiteside puffed gingerly on the thin little cigar clamped between her teeth. She enjoyed the smell and texture of cigars, but the taste they left behind and the stale smell on her fingers always reminded her she should probably quit.

Taylor cupped the glass of beer between her bearlike hands as if it were extremely fragile, and she shifted a little on the lumpy barstool. She enjoyed coming to the remote little tavern every once in awhile. It reminded her of her small-town prairie roots, where the corner tavern was the focal point of the entire community. And she could pretty much blend in with the crowd, since people from the academy rarely found their way here.

She dropped an ash in the plastic ashtray and swiveled slightly toward the tiny dance floor. A middle-aged couple danced close to the final bars of "Blue Eyes Cryin' in the Rain," their beer bottles firmly glued to their right hands. Beyond them, a young woman intently studied the jukebox.

Is that . . . ? Nah, it couldn't be.

Taylor strained harder. The young woman absently ran her left hand through her short brown hair before she punched a button. Her jeans clung to her solid, shapely legs; a black turtleneck sweater hugged her wide shoulders and firm, braless breasts.

Taylor grinned. *Holy shit, Miranda McCauley! Bright Eyes herself in a dump like this!*

"Crazy, I'm crazy for feeling so lonely," Patsy Cline crooned from the jukebox speakers.

This night's looking better and better every minute, Taylor thought smugly, ravenous eyes following Miranda back to her corner booth beneath the neon Labatt's sign.

Taylor stubbed out the remains of her cigar and drained her glass. She let the alcohol warm her stomach before she got to her feet. Yes, Miranda's just what the doctor ordered for a lonely Saturday night. It'd been a couple of months since her last conquest — a small, blond, very sexy young woman who was probably right now walking the beat somewhere in Ottawa's bar district.

"So, your first weekend at police college, and where do you spend it but at Mickey's Tavern."

Miranda looked up incredulously at the burly, grinning woman before her.

"Are you crazy, woman?" Taylor laughed.

Miranda didn't breathe. She didn't dare. She couldn't believe it was Taylor Whiteside standing just inches from her. After what seemed like minutes, Miranda shyly grinned in return and drew in a deep breath, letting the air suck away the fuzziness in her head.

"I might ask you the same, Sergeant." Despite the nervousness gnawing at her stomach, she'd play this cool, even if it killed her.

Not waiting for an invitation, Taylor slid into the seat across from Miranda. "Just call me Taylor. We're not on campus. And to answer your question," she shrugged, "what else does an old broad like me have to do on a Saturday night? You, on the other hand," she winked, "a looker like you ought to be painting this town red — or lavender at least." Her smile was almost a leer now, her eyebrows dancing suggestively.

Miranda confidently held the suggestive look, searching Taylor's blue eyes. Their shade was lighter now than Miranda remembered, and there was something mischievous, maybe even dangerous, in them.

"I'm more into quiet evenings."

Taylor looked away for a moment. "A couple more drafts here, Betty."

"So," Taylor continued, "why are you here? This place isn't exactly on the tourist brochures."

Miranda glanced away. "I, ah, just felt like disappearing for a bit."

"Do you still?"

Miranda mirrored Taylor's burning gaze, her confidence building. "No . . . not anymore."

Two full glasses appeared on their table, and Taylor paid.

There was no doubt in Miranda's mind. She wanted this woman badly. The intensity of her desire instantly melted any sexual inhibitions she might have been harboring. It was time to grow up, and Taylor would be the perfect teacher. But the nagging question lingered. Did Taylor want to be? Did Taylor want *her*?

"I hear you're a good basketball player," Taylor offered.

"Yeah, I like basketball." Miranda played coy before switching gears. If she wanted this woman tonight, she'd have to make her move soon — the shot clock was ticking down. It was clutch time. She mustered up her courage.

"What sport are you good at, Taylor?"

Impressed, Taylor licked her lips at the full-course meal about to be served up.

"Well," Taylor considered, a smile playing across her lips, her voice smoky and suggestive. "Let's just say team sports aren't my forte. I prefer one on one."

Miranda let the double entendre hang in the air, neither acknowledging nor ignoring it. Oh, yeah, she was holding her own here, no doubt about it.

"Well, then, I'll bet you know a thing or two about pool," Miranda said, nodding at an empty pool table across the room.

"As a matter of fact I do. Wanna play with me?"

Miranda smiled at the extra oomph to the word *play*.

With their beers in tow, Taylor and Miranda claimed the pool table, each picking up a cue.

"I'm afraid I'm not much good at this," Miranda apologized.

"That's okay." Taylor was serious. "I like teaching people new things."

Oh, *I hope so,* Miranda thought. She looked down at the pool table, easily picturing herself lying naked on the green felt as Taylor's tongue left a glistening trail down her flat belly.

With a crack, Taylor's cue smartly sent the triangle of shiny balls scattering across the table. Like the balls, Miranda herself felt about to explode. A blue one chased a green one into a corner pocket as Taylor began expounding on the rules of solids versus stripes.

When it was Miranda's turn, she cautiously lined up her cue. But her poke at the white ball was a misfire. She'd shot a blank. "See, I told you I wasn't any good."

"Ah, now don't give up so easily," Taylor playfully chided. "Here, let me show you."

Taylor moved behind Miranda. She wrapped her arms around her and placed her hands on Miranda's hands. It was reminiscent of the self-defense classes, only now Taylor's hands were gentle, soft. Taking her time, she guided Miranda's trembling hands to line up the cue. Having Taylor so close to her left her feeling tingly all over. How long she could maintain her cool she didn't know.

"That's it. Make sure you've got a firm hold now." Taylor's warm hands swallowed up Miranda's. "Then when you've got a good line, just give it a good whack." The cue smacked the ball and sent it careening off another.

But Taylor wasn't moving. Taylor's warm breath tickling the back of her neck, Miranda finally felt Taylor's smooth cheek brush against her own.

"I get bored with games," Taylor whispered in a slow cadence, letting the heat build. She breathed slowly and evenly into Miranda's right ear. "I think we both know what we want, and it isn't being here."

Miranda felt a throbbing ache between her legs pulsating in sync with Taylor's hot breath on her neck. She turned her face slightly into Taylor's cheek, feeling like she might pass out at any second.

"Let's get out of here."

The neon VACANT sign loomed closer and closer as Taylor's shiny black Cobra Mustang sped toward the Four Corners Deluxe Motel. The short drive had been shrouded in silence, each woman feeling the other's desire without the need for words.

Miranda waited beside the car as Taylor disappeared inside to register. She closed her eyes and sucked in the cool night air, feeling the flame still burning inside her stomach. The evening's events had unfolded quickly and, for the first time, she wondered if she wasn't imagining it all. Could it be that in minutes she would be in Taylor Whiteside's arms, unleashing a lifetime of pent-up ecstasy?

The jingle of keys wrenched her from her thoughts. Taylor was waving the room key in her face, a slow grin spreading across her face. "C'mon, Bright Eyes, we've got some business to do."

The little room obviously hadn't been redecorated since the early seventies. The bedspread sported a multicolored flower pattern, and the wallpaper was a velvet gold. The saffron lamps were just as garish.

Taylor slipped behind Miranda into the room, pushing the door shut with her back. They let their jackets slip to the floor. Taylor grabbed Miranda's right wrist, gently pulling her to her.

"C'mere, baby."

Miranda threw her arms around Taylor's neck as their mouths met without hesitation. The older woman's tongue penetrated her mouth, darting in and out seductively, playing war with Miranda's tongue and winning. Taylor's hands spread up the denimed curve of Miranda's hips and onto her firm breasts.

Taylor's body pushed Miranda's to the bed, her tongue still working its persistent mission. Miranda let herself fall back on the mattress, her arms still firmly latched around Taylor's neck as the woman hovered above. Taylor pulled Miranda's sweater up with one hand and stroked waiting nipples with the other. She finally tossed the sweater to the floor.

Miranda wanted to burst. The ache between her legs was becoming unbearable, evidenced by the spreading patch of wetness she could feel on her panties.

Taylor's tongue trailed down Miranda's neck and drew tiny circles on her chest, the circles only growing larger to encompass each breast. Miranda arched in a fervent drive to press her erect nipples into Taylor's teasing mouth. With a sly grin, Taylor inched her mouth towards Miranda's eager nipples, finally filling her mouth with them and tugging at them with gentle sucking motions.

"Oh, Taylor," Miranda gasped. "You're . . . you're so good at this."

"Am I going too fast for you, darling?" Taylor teased, pulling back.

Miranda closed her eyes, fighting off the need to explode. "Oh no, no, not at all. Please . . ."

"Please what?"

Miranda swallowed painfully, her eyes squeezed tightly shut. "Please . . . make love to me."

Taylor liked it when they begged. It only proved her superior lovemaking skills and her knowledge of what women wanted in bed. She'd built up a twenty-year portfolio in that area, and she didn't accept failure.

The stubborn button and zipper on Miranda's jeans were her next target. They quickly lost that battle as hands roughly yanked them down. Taylor's fingers dove down to Miranda's warm inner thighs, drawing soft, teasing circles that ended at her pubic hairline. Only lightly did her hand brush across Miranda's craving clitoris, almost as if by accident.

Miranda arched uncontrollably now, mouthing words that just wouldn't surface.

Right on the edge, baby, Taylor thought greedily

24

as she plunged her mouth onto Miranda's throbbing, sopping apex. Her tongue probed deep inside the moist softness, while her hands pulled Miranda's hips into her slippery face in a rhythmic dance.

Miranda could no longer cap the surging wave ripping through her body and leaving a glowing wasteland in its wake as it bubbled to the surface.

Violently, her body shook in orgasmic waves, a tumult of indecipherable words and gasps tumbling from her trembling lips.

Ah, these young ones are so quick out of the gate, Taylor smiled. Give them enough to get them begging, then watch them sprint to the finish line.

Taylor emerged from between muscular legs and lay beside Miranda, caressing her as Miranda basked in her own afterglow.

Taylor grinned smugly. "I'm sorry it was so terrible for you."

Miranda cast her luminous green eyes on the woman who was now her emancipator. If she wasn't truly smitten before, she certainly was now. She reached out and hugged Taylor tightly. "That was the most wonderful thing that's ever happened to me."

Taylor caught the almost childlike need in Miranda's eyes. Shit. She closed her eyes and stiffly reciprocated the hug. What the hell. She didn't mind the thought of Miranda depending on her, so long as she got what she wanted. It made no difference. It'd happened before and she'd always gotten out of it unscathed.

Miranda pulled back suddenly and straddled Taylor.

"Now it's *my* turn!"

Taylor laughed, seeing the same determination in

Miranda's face that she'd seen in class when the young recruit set her mind on learning a new maneuver.

Without direction, she began unbuttoning Taylor's denim shirt, then reached behind to unhitch her bra.

Miranda felt a little clumsy, but as she took Taylor's left breast softly into her mouth as though it were a delicate baby bird, she saw Taylor's eyes close and her head arch back. Clumsy or not, Taylor was enjoying it.

Miranda tenderly tongued Taylor's nipple, sensing it stiffen with each stroke. Then she traded, giving the other breast equal attention, her hand scooping it to push the nipple further up and into her mouth. Taylor silently stirred beneath her.

Impatiently, Taylor pushed Miranda's hand down to her crotch and held it there, grinding herself into Miranda's hand.

The kid needs work, but she's all right!

Tired of waiting for Miranda to remove her jeans, Taylor unzipped them and ripped them off herself before pushing Miranda's hand back into place.

Taking the hint, Miranda pressed firmly and let Taylor guide her hand in a quick, side-to-side motion. Miranda continued faster and harder as Taylor's body tensed approvingly in response.

"That's it, baby," Taylor groaned from deep within her throat.

She rode with it for a while before the explosion came quickly and satisfactorily. Miranda was pleased with herself. Awkward though she felt, she knew Taylor would help her improve. Or at least she hoped. A tinge of panic crept into her guts. Was this just going to be a one-night stand, or what? Had Taylor picked her up for that reason?

She felt like such a novice but hoped she'd been good enough to keep Taylor interested. Her crush was reaching mammoth proportions now.

CHAPTER THREE

Miranda dragged herself hollowly through the next few days. Luckily for her, she was a bright student and didn't have to put half the effort as some of her classmates into studying. She drifted from lecture to lecture, visions of Taylor taunting her. She remembered every savory detail of their lovemaking in the cheap motel. She smiled, recounting every touch, every kiss, every word. What was it Taylor had whispered to her in the bar at the pool table, her arms around her? Miranda suppressed an adolescent giggle. Oh, yeah, something about both knowing what we want... She strained to recall every precious word, every delicious detail.

It was childish, she knew, but the daily exercise was both exhilarating and frustrating. She never knew when she'd get together with Taylor next. Taylor kept a pretty spontaneous schedule it seemed, and she didn't like to divulge her plans from one day to the next.

Equally as disconcerting to Miranda was having to keep her new relationship totally under wraps. She couldn't even discuss it with her most trusted new college friends. She feared that if anyone even guessed she and Taylor were lovers, it could ruin both their careers. Sure, it was the nineties, but things weren't that liberal, especially in the male-dominated, conservative world of policing. Being an out lesbian could be an unshedable anchor to a career. They couldn't fire you for being gay, but they could sure see to it you remained a constable for good. And waiting for backup at a serious call might start taking a lot longer than it should.

Miranda had heard horror stories like that, but right now she didn't want to think that far ahead. She only wanted to think about the next time she and Taylor would be together again.

Miranda had lapsed into one of her daydreams one afternoon on the basketball court in a pickup game against B-Class. The coed games against other recruit classes were designed to promote the teamwork and brotherhood aspect that police officers, like soldiers, needed on the streets and in the battlefield.

But Miranda was especially disjointed because Taylor had volunteered to ref the game.

Sprinting into the offensive end dribbling the ball, Miranda deked and spun around, ready to plant herself for a running layup the way she'd done a million times before, when she obliviously steamrolled right through an opposing player.

The collision sent the young woman sailing backward and landing with a sickening thud on the polished floor. Shorter and slimmer than Miranda, Miki Paxton had taken the brunt of the hit, while the solid Miranda barely flinched.

"Oh, geez, I'm so sorry," Miranda gasped, running to the fallen player as the dropped ball rolled lazily away.

A circle of sweaty players gathered around as Miki slowly opened her gray-blue eyes, blinking long, pale lashes. Gently, she lifted her head and gave it a shake as if to clear it, her shoulder-length blond hair splaying out around her. Slowly, almost agonizingly, she visually took stock of herself without moving, making sure all the pieces were still attached. It was almost comical as she lifted one arm, then one leg at a time, testing each.

"Are you okay?" Miranda asked as she knelt down, annoyed with herself for forgetting where she was and who she was playing against.

"Take your time, Paxton," advised Taylor. "Everybody move back a little, okay?"

Propping herself up with slender hands, Miki smiled, her finely featured face softening as the group collectively sighed its relief.

"You'd think I was half dead or something by the look on your faces," Miki laughed, shattering the tension. Tiny dimples formed at the corners of her mouth.

Miranda forced a laugh too as the group broke up. Lending a hand to help her up, Miranda introduced herself to the fallen player. "Miranda McCauley. And I'm truly sorry. I wasn't paying attention."

Still chuckling, Miki pulled herself up and returned the introduction, looking into the most brilliant green eyes she'd ever seen. "It's okay. I should know by now to stay out of the way of people who are bigger than me."

Miranda was struck by the woman's infectious smile and quickly found herself smiling, too. Looking into Miki's dancing eyes, Miranda mentally etched the face in her mind. The woman was attractive, no doubt about that, but a little on the fragile side. In competitive ball, the play would have just continued on and the injured player would have quickly hobbled off for a substitution.

"You okay there, Paxton?" Taylor inquired.

"Yeah, no problem. It's just inspired me to score the winning basket."

Taylor grinned, then focused her attention on Miranda with a mock frown, eyes narrowed to slits. "And you, McCauley! This isn't university ball, ya bully." Breaking into a smile, she winked at Miranda and whispered menacingly. "Fifty laps for you after class."

Watching the interlude with curiosity, Miki thought back to a couple of days earlier, when she had seen Miranda going into Taylor's little cubicle of

31

an office. Not that it was unusual for a student to see an instructor after class, but it did strike her as odd that Miranda had looked carefully up and down the hall before entering Taylor's office, not having noticed Miki just rounding a corner.

That wasn't the first time she'd noticed Miranda. Miki actually remembered seeing her on orientation day and had studied her from a safe distance at drill practice the first week. Something about her had left a lasting impression with Miki. The confident posture, her direct mannerisms, her hesitant smile all pointed to the tenacity she exuded in everything she did — like her single-mindedness on the basketball court minutes earlier. It was that intensity that sparked Miki's curiosity. That and those fabulous eyes!

Miki pretended to fumble with her gym bag at the end of the game, watching Taylor and Miranda in a whispered huddle interrupted only by laughter. Moments later a smiling Miranda left for the locker room.

Miki hesitated. Something was going on. Miranda seemed so serious, so driven all the time. Yet around Taylor Whiteside, she acted almost adolescent. There was a definite distractedness about her.

That evening, Taylor and Miranda drove to a small but cozy diner on the edge of the city. With corny pop music from the sixties and seventies providing the background, they dove into their steak and potato dinners, the air crackling with the anticipation of what would happen later. They ate quickly.

Would they go back to the little motel where they'd consummated their attraction the week before? Miranda silently wondered. Or maybe another motel? Perhaps Taylor would actually take her back to wherever she lived. She didn't even know where Taylor lived — a condo somewhere in the city, she'd heard. In fact, she didn't know much at all about the mysterious older woman across from her. They'd only had that one night so far. Anything else belonged to a few stolen moments around the police college.

"What're you thinking?" Taylor volunteered, her deep blue eyes probing Miranda's.

Miranda smiled, exhaling slowly. "As if you didn't know."

Taylor's eyes narrowed. "Tell me," she insisted.

Miranda's foot gently trailed up Taylor's leg across from her, expressing unspoken desire. The tablecloth provided welcome shelter.

Miranda leaned closer, feeling Taylor's pulsating desire melding with her own. A lump of excitement throbbed in her throat. Their one encounter had definitely left her hungry for more. "I was just thinking about how much I want you. How I hate all the formalities that get in the way. How I don't care if I eat or when I eat, I only want to be making love with you."

Taylor sucked in her breath and crooked an inquisitive brow. Miranda hadn't turned out to be the naive, shy virgin she had feared. Taylor enjoyed the young woman's increasing brashness. "And just what would you like to be doing right now?" she teased.

Miranda's tongue darted out to catch the melted butter about to drip off the hunk of potato perched on her fork.

Seductively, her tongue touched the warm, glistening butter, slowing licking, tasting, savoring, tickling, then retreating back to her mouth. Eyeing Taylor the whole time, Miranda finally let out an evil chuckle.

"That's what I want to be doing to you. I want to run my tongue over you and suck in your juices until there's nothing left."

Taylor's smile vanished. "Let's get out of here."

On cue, Miranda grabbed her jacket as Taylor threw cash onto the table. Miranda had never known such acute desire. She wanted Taylor more than she'd ever wanted anyone. And Taylor's reciprocal desire thrilled her to the point where nothing else mattered.

Jamming the leather-covered gearshift into first, Taylor peeled the car out of the lot and onto the darkened country road. Shrouded in silence, Miranda felt totally contented. Finally realizing what she had refused to acknowledge all her life was a huge relief. And not just admitting her lesbianism, but actually living it out with someone who wanted her just as badly. Still, her infatuation with Taylor Whiteside often left her agitated. When she was with Taylor, she felt like a high-school kid, high on her first reckless taste of sex. And when she wasn't with Taylor, she felt unsure, confused.

Taylor suddenly pulled the car over. "Wanna drive?"

Miranda nodded enthusiastically, though she hadn't thought of it. They switched seats, and Miranda shoved the stick into first.

"Give it a good go," Taylor, proud of her car, urged.

Miranda obliged, stepping on the pedal and feeling an unexpected rush from the burst of speed. Ohh, sex and speed, she smiled. Two of the most dangerous — and intoxicating — things. Miranda bit her lip and cast a sideways glance at the woman beside her. *Are you dangerous, Taylor, like this car? Fast, tough, trendy, transparent?*

"Pull off up ahead," Taylor directed. "There's a dirt path up to the right. Just follow it, but shut the headlights off, okay?"

Miranda slowed and swung the car through the narrow dirt track and into a small grassy area surrounded by bush. With the engine silenced, only their breathing was audible in the quiet coolness.

Miranda turned to Taylor in the darkness, reached over, and caressed her cheek, running her fingertips down her neck. Strands of moonlight left shadows on Taylor's face, and Miranda saw her close her eyes and arch her head back.

"I want you," Taylor whispered huskily without opening her eyes. "I want you now, Miranda McCauley."

Obediently, Miranda straddled Taylor in her seat and resumed caressing her face, sifting her fingertips through Taylor's short, salt-and-pepper hair. Her eyes still squeezed tightly, Taylor's breathing heightened as she let the younger woman's soft touches alternately electrify and soothe her body. She kept her eyes shut. She didn't want to see Miranda's eyes — those big green pools that were probably just dripping with puppy love about now.

The thought of doing it in a car shot a charge through Miranda. It had never been a fantasy of hers, but wanting someone so badly that you just couldn't wait was exhilarating. And the sense of abandonment, the tiny prospect of being caught, thrilled her.

Miranda touched Taylor's full lips, outlining them with her fingertips. Dipping her head, she began tracing the same design with her tongue, slowly, softly, before firmly penetrating Taylor's parting lips.

Taylor's mouth pushed back at Miranda's as the younger woman's hands found their way under her shirt and cupped soft breasts. Miranda's mouth was on her throat, sucking frantically.

With lightning quickness, Taylor reached down to the mechanized seat recliner beside her and pushed the button until the two were lying as far back as the seat would go, Miranda uninterruptedly tracing a wet line down Taylor's chest as she popped the buttons open.

Taylor exhaled as Miranda's wet mouth pegged erect nipples and pulled at them gently. It wasn't like her to let her young protégés be so aggressive in the sack. She liked to make love to them first. Not since Roxie had another woman taken her first, but then Rox had been different. Rox had pierced her soul like no one else ever had, or ever would again, she'd long ago vowed.

Just as she was about to turn the tables and smother Miranda's attack, the young woman's fingers were suddenly inside her. Her mouth still on Taylor's breasts, Miranda's fingers plunged harder and faster, until Taylor's hips began pumping rhythmically against her. The kid's a fast learner! Furiously, Taylor thrust herself into Miranda's slick fingers until her body jerked and spasmed. She felt herself go limp as Miranda nestled into her.

"Taylor, I really —"

"Shhh," Taylor cut her off, sensing Miranda about to say something she didn't want to hear. Pushing Miranda's head off her shoulder, she winked and smiled. "I'm going to open the sunroof, and I want you to stand up and pull off your jeans."

Perplexed but intrigued, Miranda moved off her and did as she was asked. As the smoky glass roofing mechanically retracted, Miranda then straddled the two bucket seats on her knees at Taylor's coaxing.

"What do you want me to do?"

"Just put your head out and enjoy the stars. It's such a beautiful night, I wouldn't want you to miss any of it," she snickered.

Miranda carefully pushed her head and shoulders out, letting the cool air pierce her lungs. Taylor was right, all the stars were out and it was a beautiful, crisp night — the smell of greening grass, damp wood, and spurting buds permeating the air. It felt like the spring of her life, too.

As Miranda sucked in the May freshness around her, she felt Taylor's fingers glancing up her warm thighs.

"Wow, Taylor, I had no idea . . . ," she laughed heartily.

Her heart pounding, she sucked in more air as Taylor's tongue fervently penetrated her. She was glad she was on her knees and not her feet, because her legs felt like jelly. Slowly, like a dancer, Miranda gyrated her hips into Taylor's yielding face, feeling Taylor's tongue in her one moment, the next feeling Taylor's tongue lapping up her sopping wetness in brisk strokes.

"Oh, Jesus," Miranda moaned, nearly ready to let

the geyser inside her flood out. Then Taylor's fingers were on her, gently stroking her, her tongue pushing inside at the same time.

"Oh, Taylor, yes!" she screamed out, her insides threatening to ooze out in a warm but delicious current. Trembling softly, then quakelike, Miranda gushed into Taylor's expectant mouth. Drained, she eased her weakened body back into the car. "You like?" Taylor leered.

"You have no idea!"

"Oh, I think I do."

Taylor engaged Miranda in idle small talk as the car began winding its way back toward the city lights. But Miranda grew more silent as the gnawing inside her grew. Why was Taylor so close-mouthed about her personal life? Was she involved with someone else? Was Miranda nothing more than a sex toy to Taylor, a pleasant distraction from the daily grind at the college? Just who was Taylor Whiteside?

"Taylor, are you involved with anyone else?" Miranda boldly ventured.

Startled, Taylor looked disapprovingly at her for a long moment before she answered. "No."

"I suppose you've had a lot of other women before," Miranda said, not phrasing it as a question. One part of her didn't want to know the answer. Another part of her wanted to know if she was just one of many. "I mean, you must have had some serious relationships in the past."

Taylor ignored the suggestion, growing more uncomfortable with the conversation. From inside her jacket pocket, she plucked out a slender cheroot. Passing it under her nose briefly, she slipped it between her lips and licked the end before lighting it with a silver Zippo lighter she kept on the console. Miranda sighed her impatience as Taylor inhaled, seemingly enjoying the taste and acrid smell of her cigarillo.

"What's your house like?" Miranda asked, hoping a new direction would open Taylor up.

"It's just a house, a condo actually," Taylor reluctantly answered between puffs.

"Tell me about it."

Taylor quietly reflected for a moment on the modern, three-bedroom condominium she had once shared with Rox. God, how they used to love sitting in front of the huge living-room window at night, looking out at the river below, candlelight playing off the walls, making love well into the night in front of that very picture window.

But that seemed so long ago. Now, ever since Rox left two years ago, it was just a place to sleep. Walked right out and into the arms of another woman one day while Taylor was at work. Christ, she should have seen that coming. Rox had used her, made a fool of her.

"Nothing special, three bedrooms, the usual." Taylor hoped Miranda would take the hint and drop it.

"Maybe I'll get to see it some time. I'd like that."

Taylor fumed as she puffed away, pretending to concentrate on the driving and resisting an urge to flick the radio on. No way was this kid going to manipulate herself into her house and her life. What did she think made her so special, for chrissakes.

They had reached the edge of the city now, the glow of streetlights floating past, momentarily bathing the interior of the car in pale orange.

Miranda's impatience surged through her in waves; her face warmed. She couldn't stand Taylor's aloofness anymore, especially not after what they had shared in the car moments earlier and a week ago at the motel. She had trusted not only her body to Taylor, but she had gambled a little bit of her soul as well. She had given Taylor a piece of herself, and yet the woman seemed to take no notice that anything significant had happened.

"Taylor, why don't you ever talk to me?" she burst out angrily. "I mean really talk to me! Am I just a piece of ass to you, or what?"

Taylor was momentarily stunned. She was used to this sort of outburst once her conquests realized that sex was the motivation behind the relationship. It just usually wasn't this soon. She had been able to string along the others a little longer. Was she losing her touch?

Taylor offered a curt smile. "Look, there's no reason to get upset. Why are you trying to force this thing into something more meaningful? I mean, look, we've had sex a couple of times. It's not like we're married for chrissakes." Taylor frowned in the darkness. Jesus, these young ones think sex is a religion or something. Fuck them and they expect your soul on a silver platter.

Miranda was confused, and as though reading Taylor's mind, felt ashamed of her youthfulness and inadequacy. Taylor was right. She was being childish associating sex with commitment. She just wanted a little something from Taylor that would stem the hurt and insecurity she was feeling.

"Don't you at least like me?" she asked timidly, almost pleading.

Taylor eased the car up to the curb outside Miranda's residence building at the police college. Jerking the brake handle, she let the powerful engine idle.

"Of course. I wouldn't be with you if I didn't. But look. In another ten weeks, your course will be done and you'll be two hundred miles away in Hooperstown. What more do you want me to say?"

Miranda subdued the welling in her chest. "You just make it so difficult..." She didn't finish her thought, too proud to.

Taylor tossed her cigar butt out the window, sighed, and hollowly surveyed Miranda. She didn't owe the kid anything, dammit.

"Will I see you again?" Miranda asked tentatively.

"Of course," Taylor lied, stalling.

Three stories up, Miki Paxton stood in her darkened window watching the idling black Mustang at the curb below. She could see two shadows inside, a couple in obvious discussion.

Moments later, the passenger door opened, and a well-built young woman with short dark hair emerged. Miki blinked in surprise. Miranda! But who was she with? The tinted glass was too dark to see through.

The car sped off, with Miranda standing on the sidewalk staring at the dissipating exhaust. Miki just caught the personalized, glowing license plate before the car disappeared: TW—OPC. Hmmm, Taylor

Whiteside — Ontario Police College. Miki shook her head, a bad taste forming in her mouth. She watched Miranda walk toward the building. How strong and sexy, Miki thought lustily, her heart nesting in her throat. Miranda was the most attractive woman she'd seen in a long, long time. *What the hell is she doing with a user like Taylor Whiteside?*

CHAPTER FOUR

The next morning, Taylor took the stairs to Commissioner Ed Carter's office, having first changed from her habitual tracksuit to her uniform — a rare occasion. Carter was in charge of the college's operations, and being summoned to his office was unusual.

"Taylor," he greeted her in his deep, sepulchral voice, his hand extended.

"Good morning, sir," Taylor smiled, firmly shaking Carter's hand and taking a seat across from his oak, glass-topped desk.

Carter folded his lanky frame into his leather chair and rested clasped hands behind his balding head.

"I understand you're doing your usual good work here at the college," he smiled.

Taylor didn't answer. She didn't know what, if anything, Carter expected her to say. Was he on some kind of fishing expedition or was he simply making conversation?

Carter's crooked smile faded. "As you know, John Naiman's contract as head of the fitness department ends next month. He's returning to his force." Carter hesitated, studying Taylor. "I want you to consider being our permanent fitness and training head."

Taylor let the offer sink in. The college had never had a permanent fitness and training department head, so she had never even considered moving up from self-defense and martial arts instruction. She was pleased her five years of work at the college were being recognized.

"Well," she sputtered, flattered but surprised. "I, ah, I'd have to give it some thought. I didn't realize ..."

"Of course," Carter smiled again. "I know it may be a bit of a surprise. But these forces are getting touchy about lending us their best to teach and administer here. You know, cutbacks," he waved a slim hand in the air. "They're finding themselves short."

Carter reached for a pipe resting in a large glass ashtray on his desk and tapped the bowl three times. From his desk drawer, he pinched a wad of cherry tobacco from a pouch and tamped it into the bowl. Clamping the stem between his teeth, he lit the pipe with a long, gold lighter, breathing the tobacco to life.

Taylor inhaled the sweet tobacco odor, enjoying it vicariously.

"You're our best, Taylor," he finally continued between puffs. "You've got the training in all the fitness areas and you know your stuff better than anyone I've seen. I want you to take hold of the department and make it into the best police fitness training department in the country."

As head of the department, all the physical training of the cadets, including weaponry, would be under Taylor's auspices. All academic instruction fell under another administrator.

Carter suddenly leaned forward, his pipe in hand and his brown eyes fixed earnestly on her. "I want our officers to leave here the best-trained in the world. And you're a big part of that goal, Taylor."

Taylor was impressed, her ego enjoying the massage.

"I'm flattered, sir. And I share that goal." Taylor pursed her lips. She didn't want to appear weak, but she wanted to be sure she got what she wanted.

"My only concern is that I think I would miss teaching. I don't want to lose contact with my students by sitting behind a desk all day."

Carter sat back again, a smile of relief spreading over his craggy face. Waving the pipe in the air, he reassured Taylor. "There's no reason why we can't arrange for you to continue teaching a few hours a week."

Taylor nodded, satisfied. Though she had long since dismissed the idea, she could now easily picture herself behind a desk, more gold brocade added to her uniform, her title elevated from sergeant to inspector. She liked that. It gave her a welcome sense of renewal. She'd lost her drive for climbing the ranks since she'd left the RCMP five years back and joined the college staff.

Taylor stroked her chin, familiar bitterness throbbing in her neck. She'd given twelve years to the Mounties. In fact, she had been one of the handful of women the RCMP hired for the first time ever in 1974. But she'd hit the proverbial glass ceiling after making corporal, and her pride in wearing the red serge quickly lost its starch in the good-old-boy, quasi-military institution.

Taylor swallowed her rancor. Being made an inspector would bring changes, and not all of them welcome. "Fraternizing" with her students would have to be curtailed — it would just be too risky. She could afford to be a little reckless before, when she didn't care about promotions. Now she'd have to keep her distance.

She thought of Miranda. Too bad. But the kid was getting a little too close for comfort anyway.

The weekend was one of misery for Miranda. It was her second weekend at the college, and both had been consumed by thoughts of Taylor Whiteside. But this time those thoughts were much more disconcerting.

Taylor had promised her they'd get together again, but she'd had a funny tone when she said it. If only Miranda could be alone with Taylor for a few minutes, she'd tell her how sorry she was for acting foolish, for demanding some kind of commitment so soon. What did she expect, she chided herself, that Taylor would fall in love overnight or something?

She had no way of getting in touch with Taylor to ask forgiveness; the instructor wasn't in the phone book. Tormented with self-doubt, Miranda knew she'd have to wait out the rest of the weekend until she could hunt Taylor down on campus.

It wasn't long into Monday before she caught Taylor alone in a hallway near her office.

"Taylor, can I talk to you for a minute?" Miranda's eyes pleaded.

"Look, I'm real busy, Miranda. I have to be on the other side of campus in five minutes."

Taylor was curt and her eyes darted about impatiently. Knowing her chances were limited, Miranda started in on Taylor, deliberately raising her voice.

"I just wanted to tell you how sorry I am about the other night. I never meant to —"

Taylor grabbed her by the elbow, her face hardening into a scowl. "We're not discussing this here, you got it?"

"But I've got to get this off my chest, Taylor. The thought that you and I —" Miranda began imploring loudly. She had to subdue a smile at the success of her tactic.

"What the hell do you think you're doing?" Taylor cut in harshly, ushering Miranda to her office a short distance away.

"Are you trying to fuck both our careers?" Taylor raged at her once the door was closed. Her face had reddened into a stiff mask of barely-concealed fury, her eyes turning from dark blue to violet.

The intensity of Taylor's ire surprised Miranda, its sting smarting her.

"Look, kid, you've been begging for the truth all along. You want it so bad, well by god you got it, babe!"

Miranda swallowed hard, knowing she'd pushed the woman too far. This wasn't at all what she expected. Now, she just wanted to get the hell out of the tiny office, but Taylor's broad frame was backed against the door.

Taylor lowered her voice, which was still thick with acrimony. "You were just a good lay for me, all right? You're young and attractive. I wanted you and I got you. End of story. If you thought we were going to ride off into some sunset together, you're sadly mistaken."

Miranda swallowed a sob. Taylor was smiling now and shaking her head. How could she be so cruel? She was enjoying this, for godssakes! Miranda felt sick with hurt; tears threatened. She had to get out before they spilled over. She wouldn't let Taylor have the satisfaction.

"Poor Miranda McCauley. Just an innocent," Taylor sizzled. "A little baby dyke not ready to play with the big girls yet!"

Brusquely, Miranda shoved Taylor aside and ran out the door. Sprinting down the hall, she thought she heard Taylor laughing in the distance.

Miranda retreated into herself, unable to reveal her hurt to anyone, even to herself. Taylor had crushed and humiliated her. But it was nothing, she told herself in futile consolation. Just a fling that turned a bit ugly. It was nothing to carry on like a child about. Maybe Taylor was right. Maybe she wasn't ready to play with the grownups.

She buried herself in her schoolwork, spending long hours in the library or at the tiny desk in her room, immersed in books. And when she wasn't studying, she jogged or worked out with weights, half in the hope of running into Taylor at the gym. It wasn't that she expected a reconciliation — days had gone by since their falling out, and Taylor hadn't even attempted to make contact. They avoided each other as much as possible and were curt to each other in Taylor's self-defense class. But if Miranda could catch her alone again, maybe, just maybe, Taylor would show some remorse, or some kind of feeling. Maybe they could at least set the record straight.

Miranda's friends Vicki and Cheryl had become concerned about her quiet aloofness, but their inquiries and their attempts to draw her out met with polite obstinance. From a distance, Miki had noticed too, and instinctively she knew Taylor had to be at the root of it.

How could Miranda fall for that? Miki wondered. Taylor was so transparent. Yet, when you're alone and far from home, things can happen, she conceded. She kept her distance, knowing Miranda needed time. Crowding her right now would only alienate her. But Miki was impatient for more. She wanted to get to know Miranda, she wanted to be her friend. Hell, who was she kidding. She wanted to be her bedmate.

So it was with disappointment that Miki simply returned Miranda's brief salutations in the corridors or on the parade ground during drill practice. She pretended not to notice the pain on Miranda's face or her introspective manner.

Strapping on her protective glasses and headphones, Miki pressed the wood-plated grip of the .38 caliber Smith & Wesson revolver into her leather holster, making sure it was snug. She had been issued the standard police gun for target practice today. She wouldn't actually get her own until after graduation.

Miki entered the target range, a long narrow room with a dozen targets set up and an equal number of small Plexiglas partitioned stalls from which to shoot. It looked almost like a bowling alley.

Behind the targets was a thick wall of rubber to absorb the bullets.

A couple of other recruits were firing rounds from either end of the room. She was pleasantly surprised to see that Miranda was one of the two, down at the far end. She couldn't have planned a chance encounter better had she tried.

Miki smiled, and as she drew closer to Miranda, her heart tugged at her. She could feel Miranda's hurt. And girl, did she know just the cure!

Miranda's eyes were fixed in concentration on the target before her — the life-sized silhouette of a man's figure with white circles around the chest and head — as she blasted away. She looked wonderful, Miki thought as she eagerly studied Miranda's profile: lips pursed in steely resolve, nose straight and finely chiseled, high cheekbones a healthy pink. Like Miki, she was wearing her uniform: midnight-blue pants with narrow red stripes along the outer seams, black leather gun belt, and a short-sleeve, crisp, baby-blue shirt, the collar starched. The Hooperstown Police shoulder flashes were new and shiny. A dark tie and shiny black parade boots rounded out the standard dress.

Miki's uniform was identical but for the shoulder flashes, though she realized she didn't look nearly so compelling as Miranda did in her uniform. Miki inhaled deeply. Oh yes, baby, Dr. Paxton is in!

Miranda didn't seem to notice as Miki took the stall next to her. Miki removed her .38 and fired off the six rounds. Four of them hit the silhouetted target. As she shook the six empty cartridges from the cylinder, she stole a glance at Miranda, who was reloading her own gun.

"Hi, Miranda," she yelled over the partition, removing her headphones at the same time.

Miranda looked up from her chore, slamming the reloaded cylinder back into place. She, too, removed her headgear.

"Miki," she smiled, though it seemed forced. "How are you?"

"Better. My bruises have almost faded," Miki grinned.

Miranda relaxed her taut smile. "I'm so sorry about that. It was such a stupid thing to do. I don't know what I was thinking."

Miki laughed. "Don't worry about it. I'm only teasing you."

Miranda shook her head as if to rid the sullenness that hung over her like a cloud. "I'm glad to see you're not holding it against me." Her face had softened, but her eyes remained dark and detached.

"On the contrary." Ohh, she'd like to hold something against Miranda's body all right. "Look, tomorrow's Friday. Why don't you take a break from all your work and we'll go out for a drink in the evening?"

Miranda remembered the last time she went out for a drink — it had been three weeks since she ventured out to Mickey's Tavern and met up with Taylor. She cast her eyes down, remembering the simmering lust she had felt as they played pool. Then at the motel, Taylor's making vigorous love to her, her tasting Taylor, tasting a woman for the first time. The smell of sex and sweat lingering sweetly in the air, the warm, saggy bed they'd shared until dawn. She couldn't shake her melancholy.

"Are you okay, Miranda?" Miki had come around and gently placed a hand on her arm. "You seem awfully lost."

"Sorry, I — I'm fine." She took a deep breath. "I think I'll just stay in tomorrow night though, but thanks."

Miki tried to disguise her disappointment. "C'mon, you need a break from your work. It'll be fun, and we won't be late. I promise."

Miranda shrugged, unable to come up with an excuse. And she really didn't have the energy to argue.

"You look like you could use a drinking buddy." Miki's gentle smile was persuasive and her eyes held Miranda's. Her suggestion offered a hint of understanding.

"Well, I guess one or two won't hurt."

"That's the spirit. Come down to my room at eight. I'm on the floor right below you."

CHAPTER FIVE

Miki stood before the mirror in the tiny dorm washroom, wiping away the leftover steam from her recent shower. For the fourth time in about fifteen minutes, she brushed her silky, shoulder-length blond hair. She looked at it in disgust and stuck her tongue out at her reflection. Why did it have to lose its natural wave tonight of all nights?

She applied a faint layer of rose-tinged lipstick, the only makeup she needed. She had a healthy, natural look, and thick, long eyelashes. And tonight she felt that familiar glow, the kind she involuntarily emitted when she was sexually attracted to someone.

Her closest friends teased her about it. "And whose bones are you hoping to jump tonight?" they would laugh. Those who didn't know her so well would sometimes comment on it too, though they probably thought she'd had a couple of drinks, or maybe a good screwing. Miki smiled at the thought.

She critically surveyed herself in the mirror again. She cupped her breasts through her black silk vest, checking their firmness, then dared to unbutton one more button of her cream-colored blouse, just enough to hint at the delicate swelling of her breasts below.

Geez, she was acting like a teenager getting ready for a big date or something. She felt almost giddy.

Miki's jeans clung seductively to her trimness. She sighed, hoping she hadn't laid it on too thick. Did she look too femme? she wondered doubtfully. After all, Miranda obviously seemed attracted to the more masculine look if Taylor was any indication. Miki just didn't have the build or the strong face to pull that look off successfully.

She drew in her breath. Maybe she should remove the tiny pearl earrings. Her perfume became her next target. Hastily, she dampened a facecloth and dragged it across her neck, but she could still weakly smell the Giorgio.

A knock interrupted her ritual of self-doubting. It was two minutes after eight.

Miki flung open the door. "Hello, Miranda," she smiled eagerly, then reminded herself to keep her exuberance in check.

"Hi." Miranda scanned the empty room. "Your roommate gone for the weekend?"

"Yeah, pretty well the whole floor is. Are you ready?"

"Sure. Where're we going?"

"Oh, just a place my roommate told me about."

Miki's smile hadn't dimmed once since Miranda arrived. She couldn't help it, nor could she help the persistent tickle in her throat that made her want to giggle. She felt inebriated by the woman before her. Miranda looked more beautiful than she could have imagined. Her light brown hair had begun to show wispy highlights of blond from the warming May sunshine, and her stunning green eyes looked more lively than usual, not dull and distant the way they had the past week.

Miranda was wearing jeans, a mauve silk shirt, and a simple square-cut dark blue blazer with the cuffs rolled up to just below her elbows. Miki's pulse quickened at the broadness of Miranda's shoulders, the thickness of her legs beneath the denim. Hmmm, must be spending more time at the gym. Miki grabbed her brown leather jacket. "We'll take my car."

"That's good, because I don't have one here," Miranda laughed, glad for the pleasant distraction of Miki. She hardly knew a thing about her fellow cadet, but her natural joviality lifted Miranda's spirits.

They drove the short distance in the rain, the thwack of the windshield wipers going unnoticed as they chatted about their respective police forces.

"You probably know all about Toronto, so tell me about Hooperstown," Miki enthused. "What's it like?"

"It's kind of a quaint little town. It's a city, actually, but it's so small, I think of it as a big town.

I've only been there a few months, so I really don't know much more than the tourist brochures."

"I hear the skiing is wonderful up there."

"Yeah, it is. I squeezed in as much as I could before spring. Do you ski, Miki?"

"Oh, I love skiing. But I don't do much of it anymore. I have to watch my knee." She patted her right leg as they got out of her hatchback and walked toward the noisy building. The rain had eased to a cool mist.

"What's wrong with it?" Miranda asked, concerned.

"I did some major ligament damage when I was fifteen."

"Skiing?"

"No," Miki hesitated, a trace of embarrassment creeping into her voice. "You see, I used to be a figure skater, and —"

"No kidding?" Miranda grinned.

Miki rolled her eyes. "I know it sounds stupid, a figure-skating cop." She laughed good-naturedly along with Miranda. "But anyway, I was at the junior nationals in Calgary when —"

"You made it to the nationals?" Miranda was incredulous. That was quite an accomplishment.

Miki smiled. Shy about her skating past around jocks like Miranda, she had been hoping to play it down. She knew Miranda had been a high-school track star and an all-Canadian basketball player at the university because she had discreetly asked around at the college.

Miranda touched her arm, slowing their pace. "I think that's really great, I mean, that you made it to the junior nationals. That's really something. I can kind of see how you could be a figure skater."

"What do you mean?" Miki asked, a little defensively.

"Well, you know, I mean, you're athletic looking, but . . ."

Miki suddenly broke into laughter, the heavy bass and drumbeats of the music growing louder as they neared. "I know, I know. I'm built like a skater — small and geeky, right?"

"Smallish, yes. Geeky, no. But don't take it as an insult." Miranda mentally smacked herself for her earlier insensitivity. Another cop doesn't like to be made to feel small or weak. Miki was only three inches shorter than Miranda's five-eight. And though Miki was probably a good twenty-five pounds lighter, she didn't strike Miranda as weak. She was just smaller boned. "Skaters are strong," Miranda backpeddled. "Wiry strength, that's all. So tell me about your knee."

They entered the darkened bar, lit only by the pulsating red, orange, and purple fluorescent spotlights mounted above the corners of the spacious dance floor. There was a lull in the music as the two claimed an empty corner table.

"I was going for a triple Axel," Miki continued. "It was just a fluke thing, and I twisted the shit out of my knee. The real downer was it happened while I was warming up for my long program in the solo finals, and I was sitting in fourth after my short program. I thought I had a real shot." She frowned and looked away, her face in shadows. "At first I thought my life was over."

"I'm sorry, Miki." Miranda brushed her hand over Miki's wrist, lingering for a moment. "It must have been a real heartbreaker," she added genuinely. She knew what injuries do to athletes — she'd seen it enough times. She was just lucky to have escaped them herself.

But there was Miki, smiling again. "Ah, well, I had a few good cries, then I realized that I could concentrate on what I really wanted to do without the distraction of skating." Miki could still feel her wrist tingling where Miranda had touched it. It left her exhilarated and wanting more.

"And what was that?" Miranda asked, leaning forward, her eyes dark and serious.

"A doctor."

Miranda's eyes widened with new respect. At first sight, she'd pegged Miki as a fluff, a lightweight. And policing had their share of them, just like any other profession. But this woman was chock-full of surprises, and Miranda had a funny feeling there were more to come.

Miranda didn't even hear the waitress ask them what they wanted to drink until Miki's foot gently nudged her under the table.

"Oh, sorry, I'll just have whatever's on tap," she stammered. "So what made you change your mind about being a doctor?"

"I had to change my mind. After two years at the university, I just couldn't get my science marks past 80, and I knew med schools wouldn't even look at me. So I changed programs and became a paramedic." Her explanation sounded well-worn.

"Really?" Miranda was impressed. "So you were a paramedic in Toronto?"

"For five years."

"Five years? And here I thought if anything you were probably younger than me," Miranda laughed. "I guess it's just that I feel pretty old right now. So then what?"

"Here I am," Miki shrugged.

Their beer arrived, and Miranda plucked out some bills to pay over Miki's protestations.

"So why'd you want to become a cop?" Miranda persisted, impatient to know more about the enigmatic Miki Paxton.

Miki sipped her draft, her smile evaporating. She stared at the foam in her glass.

"I thought being a paramedic could take the place of my desire to be a doctor, but it couldn't." She looked up at Miranda, her gray-blue eyes moistening. "All the battered bodies, the blood . . . and there was nothing I could really do for any of them. Just cart them off to someone who *could* help, a doctor."

"But what you did was important. I mean, if you hadn't been there to get them to a doctor —"

Miki shook her head adamantly. "It just didn't cut it for me. It wasn't enough. It was just too painful a substitute. So six months ago I quit and decided to get into something completely different, to help people but in a different way. Can you understand that?" Miki seemed skeptical, as if few could possibly understand her feelings.

"Yes, I think I do." Miranda sipped her beer, flattered Miki had shared something so important.

The loud music began again, this time the heavy beat and squealing guitars in "Heart's You're All Eyes." Too loud to talk over, they drank from their glasses and watched groups of young women and men dance to the pounding from the large amplifiers.

At the bar, people shouted in conversation. Miranda watched a young man confidently swagger up to a bar stool where a leggy, miniskirted woman of about nineteen sat. It was obvious he thought himself irresistible with his dark hair gelled back and his leather tie gleaming in the flashing, multihued lights. He was flaunting his most charming grin, Miranda guessed, as he engaged the long-haired beauty in conversation. As their mouths moved, he kept leaning closer, his hand periodically touching her arm, his eyes never leaving hers.

Miranda wanted to laugh. She wondered how long it would take before the woman left with her Prince Charming and where they would go. Unwelcome thoughts of Taylor pricked her. How long had it taken them to leave the tavern and head for the nearest motel? Had they acted any better?

Miranda realized Miki was watching her, and she smiled at her, hoping Miki wouldn't think she was bored. Just as she was about to shout over the din, a tall, muscular, blond man suddenly approached their table and flashed the same come-on grin she had just seen from the dark-haired guy at the bar.

"How're you all doing?" he shouted to both, though it didn't take him long to zero in on Miki. The rock song faded, and Bonnie Raitt began crooning "Slow Ride."

"Would you dance with me, darlin'?" he asked

Miki in sickeningly sweet fashion. Miranda resisted the urge to mimic a gag.

Miki squirmed for a moment. "I don't think so, thanks."

"Aw, c'mon." He leaned closer, his big hands spread across the edge of their table, his white teeth gleaming like some toothpaste poster boy's. "We could have a great time together. I'm a real good dancer, I promise." His eyebrows waggled suggestively.

Miki shot him her most enamored smile. "I do like dancing, but not with the likes of you." She held her sarcastic smile while her eyes shot daggers through him.

The beefy young man's grin slowly vanished. "Maybe you just don't know what you're missing. Maybe what you need is a good —"

"Look, asshole, get lost!" Miki interrupted, her mouth curling down in anger, her face twitching in simmering rage.

Miranda grinned in spite of herself as she watched him huff away. "I guess you're used to that," she said to Miki, suddenly cognizant of how beautiful her friend was. It was easy to see how any man would be attracted to her. Or any woman. Miranda wondered if maybe Miki would have gone home with this guy if she hadn't been tagging along. It was easy to imagine men beating a steady path to Miki's table trying to hit on her. A twinge of jealousy poked at her, surprising her. Miranda didn't want anyone taking her new friend away for an intimate dance, or more . . .

"Do you mind if we get out of here, Miranda? That guy gave me the creeps."

The rain was pelting down hard as they ran to the car. "I know somewhere quieter," Miki panted as they got in. "I think I'll tell my roommate her bar really sucks."

"Now if I were a little younger, I'd probably think it was great," Miranda suggested.

"Well you're not exactly over the hill, you know."

"No, but I'm over that hill, thank God! Hey, how did you pass all your physicals with your knee, Miki?" Miranda asked as Miki slowly steered the car out of the parking lot, the wipers pumping in rhythm.

"My knee's pretty well healed now, thanks to my surgeon. I can mostly do what I want with it; it just can't take a pounding, like with skating."

"Geez, I hope I didn't re-injure it on the basketball court."

Miki laughed. "Would you stop beating yourself up about that? I'm okay, honest. I'm not gonna break."

Miki wondered what else Miranda was still beating herself up over. There she goes, probably thinking of that bitch Taylor, she thought, as Miranda turned her face to her rain-beaded window. She could feel the torment sweep over Miranda like the rainstorm outside. She wanted to broach the topic, to tell Miranda she was there for her, if she'd let her. She understood, and much more than Miranda could ever guess.

After a few minutes' silence they pulled into the sparse parking lot of Mickey's Tavern. Miranda hadn't noticed where they were until Miki turned the ignition off.

"I'm sorry Miki, I don't think I can go in there,"
Miranda whispered, looking away.

Miki bent her head, trying to look into Miranda's
shadowed face. She clasped her hand over Miranda's.

"Are you okay?"

Miranda nodded. "I'd just rather not go in there."

"Why not?"

Miranda didn't answer, but it was obvious it had
something to do with Taylor.

"It's okay, Miranda. C'mon, I owe you a drink."
She refused to let Miranda wallow in her misery.
She'd been through this with friends before.
Everything was a reminder of lost love if you let it.

Reluctantly, Miranda went in, careful to steer
Miki away from the table where she'd sat with
Taylor three weeks earlier.

"What do you drink besides beer, Miranda?"

"Bourbon usually."

"A double Jim Beam straight up, a draft, and a
Pepsi," Miki told the waitress before turning to
Miranda. "Hope you don't mind, but you look like
you need something stronger than beer tonight."

Just as the drinks arrived, Patsy Cline's "Walking
After Midnight" came over the antiquated jukebox.
Miranda took a long swallow of her bourbon, letting
the warm liquid burn her throat. Taking frequent
sips of her bourbon and chasing it down with a
mouthful of beer, she only half listened to the
amusing story Miki was telling about her police
vehicle operation class at the college. She watched
Miki's lips move between gulps of Pepsi. She was
grateful to Miki for trying to keep her distracted —
she must have sensed she was down in the dumps.

Suddenly worried that she was being miserable company, she tried now to bridge her aloofness. "How'd you get the name *Miki*?"

"I was supposed to be a boy," Miki laughed, her eyes so clear they seemed to twinkle. "Michael. When I wasn't, they just couldn't part with the name, so they called me Michaela."

Miranda smiled, glad Miki hadn't been born a boy. She sipped from her second glass of bourbon, feeling her face flush as the warm liquid slid down.

Unable to contain herself, Miki burst out in a peal of laughter. It was infectious, and soon Miranda started giggling uncontrollably until her sides hurt.

"What — what are we laughing about?" Miranda gasped between convulsions, clutching her sides.

"I was thinking," Miki giggled again, finally stopping for breath. "I was thinking how my parents never got the son they wanted. But," she winked with a conspiratorial grin, "someday, I just may bring home the daughter-in-law they always hoped for."

Others in the tavern stared at the two women as they laughed and pounded the table. Finally writing them off as drunks, they went back to their lonely business.

Miranda halted mid laugh and wrinkled her forehead pensively. Miki's admission finally hit her like a rock.

Miki, a dyke?

It had never occurred to her. Someone once told her gay people could instantly recognize other gays. What was it called? *Gaydar* or something like that. Yet Miki's admission caught her completely off guard.

"What, you're shocked by something I said? I

know the part about my parents expecting me to be a boy surprises some people."

Miranda laughed, her head shaking in disbelief. "You're priceless, you know that? So, your parents don't have a problem with your being . . ." She couldn't quite get the word out of her mouth.

"No, they're cool. But I came out when I was eighteen, so they've had nearly ten years to get used to the idea. What about your parents?"

Miranda was stunned. How did Miki know? Did everybody know? Had Taylor told people?

"I, ah, how —"

Miki caught the fleeting panic in Miranda's eyes. "Don't worry, you don't have a big *L* stamped across your forehead," she reassured her with a wink. "I can just tell these things, you know."

Miranda slowly exhaled, her body relaxing. "My parents don't know. I, I'm sort of a new recruit here in more ways than one."

"Well, good, glad you've finally come to your senses."

Miranda was no longer paying attention: her eyes focused on a spot toward the door, her face sagged, and she clammed up. Her body straightened.

Turning, Miki saw her too. Taylor Whiteside stood inside the door. She was with a young woman Miki didn't recognize from the college. Miki cast a stern look at Taylor, unable to hide her disgust for the woman. She refused to look away, not until Taylor saw them.

Taylor finally did. With an arrogant half smile, she nodded, then quickly turned away and led her companion to the far corner of the tavern. Miki returned her attention to her friend, who was quickly draining her glass of bourbon. It suddenly made sense why Miranda was so upset over Taylor. She must have been Miranda's first woman.

"What do you say we blow this pop stand," Miki suggested, not waiting for an answer before prodding Miranda out.

They drove back through the heavy downpour in silence, a pall heavy in the air. Miranda, her head fuzzy from the bourbon, sat slumped in emotional defeat. She was so detached she didn't even feel the cool rain soaking through her as Miki led her up to her dorm room. Miki was sliding the heavy wet jacket from Miranda's shoulders.

"Here, I've got a sweatshirt that'll fit you. You're soaked right through."

Obediently, Miranda turned around and unbuttoned her shirt, letting it drop in a wet pile on the tile floor.

Miki watched with warm anticipation as Miranda lifted her arms above her head, the muscles in her shoulders and back twitching with every movement. And her skin, it looked so smooth, so soft, so damned caressable.

With the sweatshirt on, Miranda turned. Blankly, she looked into Miki's heavily lidded eyes, totally oblivious to the lust lurking there.

"Have a seat." Miki motioned toward the bed, then pressed a cold beer into Miranda's hand. She'd retrieved a couple from the tiny refrigerator beside the bed, then shoved her roommate's metal-framed cot next to her own.

Miranda sipped in silence, her back against the wall as Miki took her place opposite her.

"You wanna tell me about it, Miranda?"

Miranda tried to focus on the ceiling, hoping it would clear her head. She just couldn't shake this Taylor thing. It was eating her inside. If only she could tell Miki, someone, but it was too risky. She shook her head.

Moving beside Miranda, Miki waited patiently, taking intermittent swigs from her bottle. Tenderly, she began drawing tiny circles on Miranda's knee. "I understand more than you think I do."

Miranda's eyes began filling, but she stifled the tears, staring unblinking at the ceiling, a fog enveloping her head.

"I know about Taylor," Miki finally whispered, her eyes searching Miranda's face. "I know all about her game. I know she hurt you."

With that, Miranda could no longer stem the flood; her chest convulsed in sobs. God, how she hated this, being so weak. It pissed her off. She should have been horrified that Miki knew, but she wasn't. She only felt a strange sense of relief. She buried her tear-stained face in her hands, unable to form any words.

Miki moved closer and put her arms around Miranda, pulling her at the same time. "I know it hurts Miranda. It's okay, just let it out. You don't have to say a thing."

Miki leaned her head against Miranda's, which was now firmly nestled into her shoulder. With her cheek she could feel every tremble, every new wave of tears. With her free hand, she stroked Miranda's soft, short hair, letting her fingers lightly caress her scalp and then the side of her neck. She felt rising anger for Taylor Whiteside, but her fury was quickly washed away by the softness of Miranda, the vulnerability, the trust she was bestowing in Miki. Miki never would have rebuffed Miranda like Taylor had. Miranda would never spill one tear over her, because she would never hurt her like this. She thought now of the old Gladys Knight song from her childhood, "If I Were Your Woman," and her heart ached for what could have been.

Reluctantly, Miranda pulled herself away, the flow of tears having finally ebbed. "I'm sorry, Miki, I didn't mean to —"

"Did anybody ever tell you that you apologize too much?" Miki reprimanded softly. With both hands she took Miranda's moist face and held it in her hands. "I want to be your friend, Miranda. You don't ever have to apologize to me for anything." Then she guided Miranda's head back to her shoulder and held her tightly.

Miranda let herself be pliant under Miki's caring hands. She felt like a small child again, curled up against her grandmother's loving bosom, rocking back and forth in the sun-bleached wicker rocker on the porch of the old clapboard house. She closed her eyes and could almost smell the salty ocean and hear the gulls in the distance. With little effort, she could nearly mistake the caressing of Miki's fingers for the warm summer breeze brushing her face, fluttering her hair. How she used to love spending summers at her grandparents' cottage on Vancouver Island.

Miki felt the rhythmic rise and fall of Miranda's chest against her. She'd fallen asleep in her arms. Brushing hair from her ear, Miki bent her head and ever-so-faintly kissed Miranda's ear, then held her lips to her forehead.

Earlier she'd wanted to jump Miranda — and still, her body demanded more — but there was a need to simply hold Miranda and protect her from everything bad in the world.

Hours later, with the early morning sunshine blinking through the Venetian blinds, Miranda stirred in the tiny cot. She awoke to feel Miki wedged up against her, her arm lazily strewn across her.

Gracefully, Miranda slipped out and rolled off the bed. Embarrassed that she had fallen asleep, she wanted to get out before Miki awoke.

At Miki's gray metal desk, she found a blank pad of paper beneath a leather-bound Criminal Code. She saw that Miki's initials were stamped in gold on the cover.

Miki: Sorry I had to leave early. I forgot to mention I was invited to my aunt's out of town for dinner tonight. Have to catch the ten A.M. bus. Back tomorrow. Thanks for everything — Miranda.

Miranda hesitantly set the pen back in its place. After a final look at the sleeping Miki, she scooped her damp jacket and shirt from the floor and slipped out the door.

The note wasn't a lie, but just the same, she felt like a shit. Miki had been so good to her last night, so understanding, so . . . loving. And here she was sneaking out like a thief in the night.

Confusion weighed even heavier now. Not in a long time had anyone held her like that. It'd felt so good, too good, to let herself go like that. But what did it mean? Was Miki just being a good friend to her? Or did Miki have other intentions? And had Miranda really felt that undeniable stirring between her legs? She inwardly recoiled. She couldn't possibly think of hooking up with anyone right now — she had neither the energy nor the desire. Though Miki was desirable, no doubt about that, and she had shown Miranda a very special side of her.

Ah, it's probably just the booze.

Stopping in the hall for a moment before the stairwell door, she leaned back and put a hand to her temple where a dull throbbing had begun.

CHAPTER SIX

Miranda returned to the college late Sunday afternoon. She hastily retrieved a handful of textbooks from her room and just as quickly made for a quiet corner in the library. On her way, she folded the sweatshirt Miki had loaned her and set it outside Miki's door, careful not to make any noise. On her way, she folded the sweatshirt Miki had loaned her and set it outside Miki's door, careful not to make any noise.

Instinctively, she knew Miki would be looking for her. But she just wasn't ready to be reminded of the weakness she'd shown. She was becoming so damned spineless lately — nothing but a wobbly bowl of Jell-O, she thought scornfully. She hated herself for having lost control of her feelings with Taylor. By god, though, it wouldn't happen again.

Miranda's thoughts wandered to Miki, and how she'd meant so much the other night. *Too much.*

Miranda closed her book and rubbed her forehead, hoping the friction would clear her head. All weekend she'd been unable to avoid thoughts of Miki. Even when she tried not to think of her, there she was anyway, like a recurring dream. Miranda hadn't known such gentleness, such raw vulnerability, such need, since she was a kid. She'd unknowingly shed that part of her along the way. Somewhere it had just evaporated, like her crayons and coloring books, like pimples and pinup posters. Yet there was Miki Paxton, gathering up those lost pieces and giving them right back to her.

She didn't need this complication right now. Taylor had been complication enough.

The mood was jovial when all four recruit classes gathered outside the next morning for their twice-weekly drill practice. Normally the two hours of marching were met with grumpiness. But it was the first of June, and they were about a third of the way into their training. The light at the end of the tunnel was emerging, if only faintly.

Miranda adjusted her cap, careful not to smudge the shiny vinyl brim. She knew she'd have to say something to Miki. It was nagging her that Miki knew all about Taylor. How had she known? She hadn't seen any obvious evidence that the two knew each other already. At least they hadn't acted that way. So how had she figured out her and Taylor's relationship?

"*Atten-tion!* " the drill sergeant bellowed.

The rows of blue shirts snapped stiffly to attention; silence was automatic.

"*Pa-rade! Ri-i-i-ght turn!* " the sergeant shouted. The columns turned as one unit and halted with a collective stomp. "By the left, *Quick ma-a-rch!* " The three long columns moved in brisk unison.

As she marched, Miranda's mind stubbornly steered to thoughts of Taylor. Who was that woman she was with at Mickey's Tavern? And was that a smirk on her face when she'd noticed Miranda? She hadn't been sure in the dim lighting.

Goddamn her! Taylor had used her like some piece of furniture to discard. No, worse than that, like a tube of toothpaste with every bit of usefulness squeezed out. But Miki, Miki had shown her the kind of compassion and understanding that Taylor should have, that any caring lover would have.

"*Hooperstown!* What fucking world are you in!" The sergeant's shrieks brought Miranda out of her reverie. She'd fallen out of step with the rest of her platoon.

Shit! Shit on a fucking stick, she swore inaudibly.

"You look like you're window shopping at the mall, Hooperstown," the sergeant uttered in put-on disgust. McCauley was one of the more disciplined recruits. What the hell was wrong with her?

Miki, a column behind, was wondering the same, knowing Miranda was one of the best in drill. She was hurt that Miranda seemed to be avoiding her.

She hadn't heard from her since Friday night, and Miranda was never in her room when Miki stopped by.

After nearly two hours of practicing precision turns and uniform marching, the sergeant barked the final fall out command.

Sweat beading on her forehead, Miranda removed her hat and began berating herself for the hundredth time for having lost her concentration. She was thinking far too much lately; she was losing touch. Her first three weeks at the college had been spent in bouts of either daydreams or self-pity, and she was sick of the whole thing.

The fling with Taylor was a mistake, pure and simple. A mistake because she'd given too much of herself. And what had she gotten for it? Nothing but a couple of cheap fucks and a broken heart. Just because Taylor was her first woman didn't mean she had to build a shrine for her.

Forget it Miranda. Forget her.

"Miranda." It was Vicki Mason, ambling her way up to Miranda.

"Hi," Miranda smiled. "Quite a workout, wasn't it?"

"Yeah," her friend panted, looking bedraggled, her face creased with worry lines. "Miranda, I really feel like I'm falling behind in Federal Statutes, and I know you've been acing that stuff. Would you help me study tonight?"

"Sure," Miranda shrugged. "I'll meet you at the library at seven."

"Hi, guys," came a familiar approaching voice.

Miranda turned. It was Miki, hat in her hands, striding toward them.

Vicki smiled. "Hey, Miki. You looked good out there. Wish I could say the same."

"You were great," Miki lied.

"Look, I gotta go. Thanks, Miranda. See ya, Mik."

Silently, the two watched Vicki join the others heading for the building. There were classes to get to.

"How was your weekend?" Miki was trying her best to sound casual, but her eyes gave away her disappointment.

"It was okay. Good to catch up with my aunt, you know. I haven't seen her in a year."

Miki nodded, her hands nervously kneading the brim of her hat. "I'm sorry I missed you when you got back."

Miranda studied the reflection in her own boots for a moment, then met Miki's inquisitive gaze. "No, I'm the one who's sorry." She drew in a deep breath, then exhaled slowly through her nostrils. "Let's go for a little walk."

Miki's silence cloaked her palpable anxiety as they walked toward a large shade tree. She couldn't stand not knowing why Miranda had avoided her. She thought they were friends.

"Miki, when I got back, I . . . I sort of tried to disappear." She was suddenly tired of games but not quite sure what to say, either.

They stopped before the tree. "I was embarrassed that I fell apart on you the way I did. It's not like me. I hate being weak like that."

Miki tried to smile, but the hurt in her eyes caught Miranda by surprise. Christ, she almost looked like she was about to break out crying.

"I'm sorry, Miki. You were so good to me, and you didn't deserve that."

"I wish you didn't feel that way with me, Miranda. Was it really that horrible opening up to me like that?"

"No, it wasn't," Miranda sighed, nervousness gnawing at her gut. Talking about her. feelings was a bit new for her, and it left her fidgety. "It meant a lot to me the way you ... the way you were there for me. No one's done that for me in a long time. I wasn't prepared for it." Embarrassed, she pretended to study the bark on the tree. "I wasn't prepared to feel the way I did."

Miki's warm smile returned. "I don't ever want you to feel badly for being yourself with me, Miranda. And I know what you're going through."

"*Was* going through," Miranda corrected. "I'm better about it now. Taylor isn't worth getting that upset over. I know that now."

Miki nodded enthusiastically. "You're right about that. I'm just glad you realize it now."

"How did you know about her?" Miranda whispered as they began their walk back.

"Taylor Whiteside's reputation precedes her. I've heard a lot about her through the grapevine."

"What, you heard she goes through lovers like underwear or something?"

Miki laughed. "Yeah, so to speak. But it wasn't until I saw her handiwork up close that I really saw what she was about."

"What do you mean?"

Miki hesitated, as if drawing on a painful memory. "What she did to you, she did the same to my ex, Beth, a couple of years ago when Beth was a recruit here."

"You mean they had an affair on you?"

"No, no. Beth and I had pretty much ended it by then, but we were still good friends. So when she came back, I was left to pick up the pieces."

"You must hate Taylor Whiteside."

Miki laughed again. "*Hate*'s a pretty strong word. But then, you could say I have strong feelings for Taylor Whiteside." Serious now, she touched Miranda's arm. "What she did to you, Miranda, it just sickens me all over again. I see the same thing in your eyes that I saw in Beth's."

Miranda stopped a few feet from the building's doors and studied her friend. There was no denying what she saw in those smoky gray-blue eyes. Miki cared an awful lot for her.

"Miranda. You said a few minutes ago, that you weren't prepared to feel the way you did when we were together Friday night. What did you mean by that?"

Damn. She hadn't meant for Miki to zero in on that. How could she just come right out and tell her how afraid she was of needing her, of emotionally depending on her? And more than that, of wanting her? Being held in Miki's arms like that was a hell of a lot more real than falling into bed with Taylor. But she'd had enough emotional somersaults to last her the rest of the year. No more falling into bed with anyone.

"C'mon. We're going to be late for class."

* * * * *

Miki spent the rest of the week vacillating between attempting a pass at Miranda and letting her go altogether. Miranda had been showing occasional signs of interest, but every time the moment even hinted of anything more, she backed off.

What was it with her? It wasn't that she seemed uncomfortable with her sexuality. Miki had been through that door before with potential lovers. Was it Taylor she was still thinking of? No, Miranda had said that much herself. Maybe she just wasn't attracted to Miki in that way.

Reluctantly, Miki made the two-hour drive home to Toronto that weekend. She brooded over Miranda and turned every moment they had spent together over and over in her mind. She desperately searched for both clues and answers. Sleep did not visit her until dawn, and even then it was erratic.

By the time she made the trip back early Sunday evening, she had firmly decided to erase any thoughts of Miranda as a lover. It just wasn't going to happen. Miranda was someplace else, and wherever it was, there wasn't room for Miki. Cranking her car stereo to the raspy rock singing of Stevie Nicks, Miki concluded her friend was simply driven by her work at the college and wasn't interested in any more emotional attachments. In a way she couldn't blame her, after all that shit with Taylor.

Taylor! Miki felt the sting of tears in her eyes as her car lapped up the miles. She'd hurt Miranda, maybe irreparably. If only Miki had beaten Taylor to it, Miki and Miranda would be together right now. It could have been so good with us, Miranda. If you just weren't so damned stubborn, you'd see that.

All Miki wanted now was for the final eight weeks at the college to pass swiftly. They would then go back to their respective cities and she could forget Miranda McCauley altogether.

After a couple of hours of studying Provincial Statutes, Miki tried without success to fall asleep. She stirred, turned over, and tried every sleeping position possible. Nothing worked. Careful not to disturb her roommate, she threw on a pair of shorts and a T-shirt. Maybe a sauna in the gym's locker room would help. It was open all night, and maybe it would rinse thoughts of Miranda away.

Miki turned up the dial just inside the sauna room to let it heat up. She retreated to the adjoining locker room to wait. On a bench was a solitary gym bag. It looked familiar somehow, but she couldn't be sure.

Curious, Miki jogged the short distance to the conditioning room. It wasn't unheard of for a recruit to take advantage of a lonely late-night workout, but it was rare for a weeknight. Maybe whoever it was had insomnia like her.

As she rounded the final corner, a pleasant surprise greeted her. Miranda! There she was, her back to the door, pumping furiously on a stationary bike. Miki smiled and stood leaning against the doorjamb, temporarily paralyzed by the delight of just being near Miranda. Desire licked at her like thirsty flames.

Miranda's bare legs glistened with sweat beneath

the form-fitting black spandex shorts. Every fiber of her thick quads and hams bulged with each turn of the pedal.

Miranda's blind concentration inexplicably broke. She slowed, then stopped, her breathing heavy but even. She had the distinct feeling that someone was watching her. Turning, she saw Miki standing there, a dazed smile on her lips. Somehow, Miranda wasn't surprised. She'd secretly hoped Miki would intercept her lonely mission one of these nights.

Their eyes met for a long moment in silent understanding before Miranda turned back to the twinkling computer screen on the bike's handlebars, her head bowed in quiet contemplation. She felt Miki slither away.

From her look, Miranda knew Miki wanted her, and she knew it was unavoidable. More than that, it was inevitable. It felt so right — so *necessary* to go to Miki now. It had to happen. Hell, ever since that first night out together, Miranda'd known deep down it would happen. And so like a toy train on its remote-controlled path, she hopped off the bike for her dance with destiny.

Wrapping a large white towel around her, Miranda stepped into the sauna and locked the door behind her. Through the clouds of foggy mist, Miki's distant, towel-clad form lounged on the wooden bench. The dim yellow glow from the light above left murky shadows on the walls. Miranda had to squint to see anything.

"Come here," came the familiar voice, demanding, though not harsh.

Miki sat up as Miranda stood silently before her,

heart racing. Reaching out, Miki's fingers found the knotted gathering of Miranda's towel. With a single deft stroke, she ripped the two ends apart and watched with pleasure as the towel fell to the floor.

"I've been waiting for this since you decked me on the basketball court," Miki whispered, pulling Miranda forcefully to her. Miranda was about to laugh at Miki's choice of words, but the urge was quickly extinguished by Miki's eager mouth.

The tugging continued until Miranda lay on top of Miki's supine figure. Miranda returned Miki's insistent kissing as fingers brushed through her damp hair, tracing her soaked hairline. Then hands, soft, slender hands, danced along her slippery back and followed muscular lines down to her buttocks. There they drifted, caressing, teasingly pinching, massaging.

With each electrifying touch Miranda's yearning flared, growing from a warm glow in the pit of her stomach to a raging fire. She ached to burst forth and draw Miki in until they melted together into a scorched heap of exhausted pleasure.

Miranda slid her mouth down Miki's neck to her breasts, her saliva mixing with the salty moistness. With Miki's arms stroking and caressing her, she felt the warmth spread from her thighs to her chest. Her throat tightened with the overwhelming emotion surging through her. She had never felt so connected, so at peace. She'd never before lost that feeling of individuality in lovemaking, where she had always been keenly aware of her own body, her own pleasure, her own mechanical need for release. This time, she got pleasure by pleasuring.

Miki's finger slipped into her and was met with

slick suppleness eager to encompass. With her other hand sliding over Miranda, Miki tickled and teased, dancing around her clitoris before finally claiming it.

Miranda raised herself slightly and slid her own hand over Miki's stomach and through the thick patch of velvety blond. There her hand cupped the yielding bulge and began vibrating back and forth. In unison, they labored for breath, rocking furiously, a salty concoction of sweat and saliva coating them.

Miki's mouth desperately latched onto Miranda's neck, pushing into her. With a violent shiver, she came first in a throaty moan. Miki's pulsating body beneath her was all the catalyst Miranda needed. Pressing her mouth to Miki's firm breast, Miranda rode the waves of orgasm as they swept over her patiently, almost serenely, promising not to subside anytime soon. She'd never come this calmly, this deeply, this slowly before. She felt as though she'd been turned inside out. And as Miki's arms tightly clasped her, she felt so safe.

"Miki, I . . . oh," she exhaled, finally giving up. She felt close to tears.

Miki pressed her head into her and stroked drenched hair. Sweat dripped from her face to Miranda's chest, trailing down along the sides of her breasts and forming little pools on the bench.

There was no need for words. Both silently explored the pleasant glow inside. After a few moments, until she feared Miranda may have dozed off on her, Miki cupped Miranda's face and gently tilted her head toward her.

"How about a shower, my sweet?"

Miranda smiled. "Only if I can wash you myself and then lick you dry."

CHAPTER SEVEN

Practically every minute outside of class, Miki and Miranda were inseparable. Their friends took immediate notice of the fast friendship and often teased them, nicknaming them M&M's after the candy.

Miki stopped going home on weekends so the two could spend them together. Sometimes this meant holing up in a hotel room with a twelve-pack of beer and a queen-size bed. When money was tight, they'd sneak to one or the other's room and sleep over, depending on whose roommate was gone for the weekend. Or they might take off in Miki's car for a long drive in the country, usually to some secluded spot.

"So tell me," Miki said on one such bucolic excursion, looking down at Miranda's tanned face as she lay sprawled on her back on the blanket. "Why did you want to become a cop?"

Miranda opened her eyes, which felt heavy under the bright, June sun. They had just finished a picnic lunch of ham sandwiches and beer, and the combination of the warm sun and cool alcohol left Miranda feeling sleepy.

She smiled, squinting from the sun. "Where did that come from?"

Miki was serious. She lay alongside Miranda, propped up on her elbow. "I just never asked before, but I'm curious. I've already told you my life story."

Miranda eyeballed the cleavage showing from Miki's loose tank top. She could see where her tan line ended and where her firm, pale breasts began their subtle protrusion. She wished she could wake up enough to yank that damn tank top up and plant her lips on those breasts.

"C'mon, let's snooze for a few minutes." Miranda closed her eyes again.

"No, no, I'm serious," Miki insisted.

A hawk circled far above, gliding with ease. The sound of the intermittent breeze rustling the tall grass was the only audible interruption. Thankfully there were no tourists around; it was still early for vacation season. It had taken Miki and Miranda about two hours to drive to the large sand dunes off the shores of Lake Huron. They were high atop one such dune, with other smaller ones forming a semicircle behind them. Tall grass sheltered them from view.

Miranda sighed. "I'm afraid I don't have a lofty mission like you."

"Meaning what?"

Miranda reluctantly pried her eyelids open again, finally giving in to Miki's persistence. "I mean I'm in this for one thing. I want to go to the very top, and I want to be the best." Miranda hoisted herself up on her elbow to face Miki, a little embarrassed by her admission. "I'm sorry if that sounds arrogant."

"No, not at all. I admire that," Miki smiled proudly, a gleam of understanding in her eye. "So you want to be chief of Hooperstown?"

Miranda was deadly serious, her energy trickling back into her. Her eyes narrowed as she stared off at some vision only she could see. "I want to be chief of the biggest force in the country." Then a shy smile unexpectedly crept across her face. "But I guess I can start with Hooperstown."

Miki smiled too, but she realized Miranda was simply trying to make light of something deeply important to her. It frightened her. Could there be room for her in the life of someone so career oriented?

"But why policing? Why not business or law or something else?" Miki pressed on, more for the sake of keeping herself from brooding than for want of an answer.

"My grandfather was an inspector with the RCMP in British Columbia. He was kind of my role model."

"Are you close to your grandparents?"

"I was," Miranda blinked. "They both died when I was a teenager."

85

"Oh, I'm sorry, Miranda."

Miki was silent for awhile. "What about your parents. Are you close to them?"

Miranda rolled her eyes. "What's with all the questions? You bucking for detective already?" she teased.

"No, I just want to know about you." Miki's eyes glowed lovingly, though Miranda pretended not to notice and rhymed off her rote answer.

"My parents are divorced. Mom lives in Montreal half the year and Florida the other half — she remarried a few years ago. And Dad lives in Vancouver."

"No brothers or sisters?"

Miranda shook her head, feeling a twinge of emptiness.

Miki reached over and stroked Miranda's cheek. Miranda was inwardly grateful for the silence.

She began returning Miki's caresses and crooked her eyebrows suggestively. "I'm a little thirsty in this heat."

"I'm sorry, I think our six-pack is all gone."

"I wasn't thinking of beer," Miranda leered. Gently she nudged Miki onto her back and climbed on top of her, hiking up the pink tank top. Her breasts were a creamy white next to her tanned chest. Bright pink nipples darkened and grew erect under Miranda's tantalizing tongue.

It seemed to Miki that Miranda was spending hours kissing and tonguing them, occasionally caressing nipples between thumb and forefinger. It was driving her wild, and Miki had spontaneously begun to grind her hips into Miranda.

"Ohh, yes," she gasped. "Make love to me!"

Miranda smiled, eager to oblige. Crouching over Miki, she yanked down her skimpy nylon shorts and beamed at what awaited her.

"Wow, no underwear! I had no idea . . ."

Miranda set down her pencil and rubbed her temples. She knew the answer she was supposed to write on the answer sheet, but still it rankled her.

She had the procedure down cold for responding to a hostage-taking situation; she had practiced it just the day before. She and three other recruits, including Miki, had responded to a mock hostage-taking exercise on campus, with the instructors scrutinizing their every move. Ignoring textbook procedure, Miranda had crawled behind a tree within a dozen yards of the old shack. She had attempted to get close to a window to pick off the "gunman" or maybe even get inside.

Miranda frowned, remembering the dressing-down and the poor mark she'd gotten for trying to be a hero. Call the sharpshooters, evacuate the area, and stay well back, she'd been reminded. And for her own benefit, the instructor offered to show her graveyards of would-be heroes.

Miranda stared across the classroom at Miki, who was furiously scribbling away. Miki, like the instructors, had given Miranda shit for her solitary heroics. No one liked a loose cannon for a partner, and Miranda had to concede that point. Plus she knew Miki only had her best interests in mind, but dammit, it had been so tempting! She could have had him!

Miranda studied Miki's shoulders hunched in concentration, then watched as Miki raised her pencil to her soft lips, knit her brows, and wrinkled her perky nose as she contemplated a question. Miranda smiled. Closing her eyes, she remembered the taste and texture of those lips, the fresh smell of sunshine on that skin, the smoothness of those eyebrows. Miranda's lips knew every delicious inch of Miki.

Just as Miranda opened her eyes again, Miki caught sight of her and winked, her eyes aflame, her cheeks flushing. Quickly, Miranda looked away, focusing on the exam in front of her. She sighed heavily. Graduation was nearing, and though she knew what she had to do, her breath caught in defiance. She'd have to steel herself for what was ahead.

Miki and Miranda held each other tightly in the darkness, happily crowded on the two cots shoved side by side in Miranda's dorm room. It was their last weekend before graduation.

"I just had the neatest thought," Miki said, breaking the silence that had followed their lovemaking.

Miranda kissed her cheek. "What's that?"

"I was about to drift off, when I had this vision of the two of us trudging through a snowy field to cut down a Christmas tree."

Miranda could faintly make out the smile on Miki's face nudged up against hers. She laughed sleepily. "A Christmas tree? What on earth would make you think of that? It's July for godsakes."

Miki sighed happily as she nestled closer. "I don't

know. But it felt great. We were so happy, just like little kids. I'd love to do that with you." She looked up anxiously at Miranda.

Miranda closed her shadowed eyes.

"Didn't you hear what I just said? I want that for us."

"Yeah, yeah, a Christmas tree. You want a Christmas tree for us," Miranda finally answered with a yawn.

Miki lightly whacked Miranda's arm in mock anger. "Not just a Christmas tree. Our tree, for our house."

Miranda felt her mouth go dry and a lump taking root in her throat. She opened her eyes again and stared gloomily at the darkness above. There was no more putting it off. This was it. She had to tell Miki. It wasn't fair to keep her dangling. No way was she going to be another Taylor Whiteside.

Miranda sat up, fluffing the pillow to support her back. She turned to Miki. "Miki, look, I think we need to talk." She reached beside her and clicked on the lamp.

Miki sat up too, her smile fading. Deep down, she knew what was coming. She'd been fooling herself for weeks, telling herself Miranda would come around and admit she loved her, admit she needed her on a permanent basis. She'd been purposely trying not to pressure Miranda and, though it was hard, she'd pretty much managed to keep her own feelings in check, at least verbally. Well, except for the couple of times she'd blindly blurted out during lovemaking that she loved Miranda. But each time the remark had met with stony silence. They simply didn't talk about it.

But it wasn't just the *L* word that seemed to freeze Miranda. Any time Miki tried to show her a bit of affection outside of bed — sneaking a little kiss or slipping her hand into Miranda's — Miranda shrank back. Exasperated, Miki had stopped, and it killed a little part of her inside to do so. Again, they didn't talk about it. Instinctively, Miki felt Miranda's fear of getting close. Probably wanted her freedom just as soon as graduation came.

"Hey, all right, forget the Christmas tree," Miki tried to laugh as tears burned in her eyes. "I know not everyone likes real Christmas trees. We could, you know . . . just hang stockings or something." Miki tried to suppress a sob, and not too successfully. "Or we could get one of those tacky little ceramic trees that light up and —"

"Miki, don't," Miranda quietly pleaded. The pitiful jokes weren't working.

Tears flowed from Miki. Miranda reached out to encompass her lover's shaking body, hating herself for being the cause of it all. She knew Miki loved her, and yet she was about to toss her away, just like Taylor had trashed her. Miranda couldn't stop her own silent tears from trickling down, but she couldn't wimp out of her mission now.

"I'm sorry, Miki. I don't want to hurt you, you know that, don't you?"

Miki nodded, her head still buried against Miranda's chest. She couldn't see that Miranda was crying too.

"Next week we're going to be in different cities. And we've got our careers to think about." Miranda was still desperately trying to convince herself as well as Miki. She had to be strong, for both of them.

"We're going on separate paths now, and our careers haven't even begun yet."

Miki didn't answer. Her sobs had subsided, but she still sniffled.

"Say something, would you?" Miranda implored, drying her face with the back of her hand.

After a few moments, Miki pulled her tear-stained face away. Her eyes were glazed and empty as they bore into Miranda.

"I'm not making any apologies for the way I feel about you." Miki was quickly regaining her composure. "I love you, Miranda, and I always will, no matter what you say you feel about me." She couldn't force Miranda to love her, nor could she trap her. But if she could, she would have.

Miki got up from the bed and began dressing. Miranda didn't want her to go — they still had a week left at the college — but she had no right now to ask Miki to stay.

"Miki, I don't want it to end like this."

"Look, I just can't pretend everything's fine. This is what you want, then this is the way it'll be."

Miki pulled her jeans up over her hips and zipped them shut, tucking her shirt tails in. She hurriedly tugged her running shoes on without tying the laces. "I love you," she whispered over her shoulder as she reached for the doorknob.

"Miki, wait." Miranda sprang out of bed and slipped into her robe. She touched Miki's arm, wanting to say something, anything that would make her stay. But no words seemed suitable.

"I love you," Miranda whispered to the closed door.

* * * * *

Graduation morning at the police college dawned sunny and hot. The dorms, like their inhabitants, were in disarray. Most of the recruits had been up late celebrating, and some had begun packing for the trip home.

By ceremony time, the graduates looked resplendent. They shone with an eager confidence, like the polished boots and gleaming buttons of their uniforms.

Piped into the gymnasium by a police pipes-and-drums band, the recruits marched in perfect precision before a beaming audience.

Miranda's mother and aunt proudly watched her called to the podium three times — the first time for a handshake and diploma, the second time to receive the award as the top graduate of her class, and a third time as valedictorian.

She was modest about it all, and her classmates respected her for it.

Miranda needed only to think of her grandfather, and the inspiration came for her valedictory address. He was everything a cop should stand for; she hoped she could be as honorable. And so she focused on personal integrity as she stood before the gathering.

Miranda scrutinized the audience before her, holding her breath all the while. Hundreds of people, maybe even a thousand, were crowded into the room. Finally, she settled her attention on her fellow recruits, since she wanted her message to reach them. She emptied her lungs slowly.

"My fellow graduates, friends, and families. Today, all of us in this room share one of the proudest moments of our lives. Let us now carry that pride into our daily working lives. May we proudly wear the badges we have earned, use the tools we have acquired, and display the courage we have yet to prove so that we may do the job we have been entrusted with. And let us reserve our deepest pride for serving the citizens of our respective communities."

The applause gave Miranda a few seconds to peek at her notes.

"We must reach out boldly and honestly to perform our new duties. And in so doing, we will face real obstacles, real dangers, and seemingly insurmountable tasks. But always must we do so in a way that preserves our own allegiance to the fundamental principles and promises of our Constitution."

Miranda looked directly into the faces of her peers, careful to speak slowly and clearly.

"My fellow graduates, our success or our failure, as police officers and as individuals, will be measured by the answers to these four questions: Did we act with courage? With integrity? With dedication? And with fair judgment?"

Miranda paused, shamefully reflecting on the pain she'd caused Miki. Had *she* acted with integrity? No. With courage? Ha! Her eyes searched for Miki among the uniforms, but she couldn't pick her out.

She ended her speech by quoting one of her grandfather's heroes, John F. Kennedy: "Prepare your heart and mind for the task ahead, call forth your strength, and let each devote his energies to the betterment of all."

* * * * *

"I'm so happy for you." Miranda's roommate Cheryl hugged her after the ceremony. "You were great up there. I know you worked hard for all this."

"Thanks. And thanks for putting up with me."

Her friend Vicki had barely squeaked through, and owed much of that to Miranda.

"I don't know what I would've done without you," Vicki smiled through tears as she hugged Miranda too.

Miranda squeezed back. "You'd have done just fine, and you'll be great. A lot of this classroom stuff is just bullshit anyway."

Vicki shook her head. "You're the one who's gonna be great. You're going to put us all to shame. Now c'mon." She tugged at Miranda's sleeve. "My mom's going to take a picture of a bunch of us." She wouldn't take no for an answer.

Miranda followed Vicki to where a plump, middle-aged woman stood meekly with a camera. On the way over, Vicki convinced a handful of others to join them.

"Hey Miki," she yelled. "C'mon over here and get your picture taken with us, girl!"

Miki, her blond hair braided and pulled up into her cap, joined Vicki, Miranda, and the others. She smiled broadly, taking great pains to mask any perceived rifts between her and Miranda. But it was obvious there was some kind of wall between them now, as Miranda shifted uncomfortably, keeping a few feet of distance between them.

"I want you two side-by-side, c'mon now. I know you're such good friends." Vicki remained steadfast until they shifted into place, the camera clicking away.

It wasn't until the gymnasium was practically empty that Miranda finally had to abandon the idea of getting Miki alone one last time. Every time she went to look for Miki, someone grabbed her arm or shook her hand one last time. She needed for Miki to understand why they had to break up. Miranda had done them both a favor, couldn't she see that?

She'd already told her mother and her aunt she'd meet them for dinner. It was getting late. *Damn, Miki must've slipped out.* Miranda walked outside and breathed in the warm air, taking pleasure in having a few minutes alone. As she rounded the corner on her way to the parking lot, she caught sight of Miki sitting alone on a cement curb.

She jogged up to her, both worried and anxious. "Are you okay, Miki?"

Miki looked up, a flash of relief and tenderness in her eyes, but it was only a brief lapse before the wall went back up. Slowly she got to her feet and brushed herself off.

"Yeah, of course I'm okay. I'm just waiting for my family to pick me up. They're going to help me pack, and then I'll follow them home."

Miranda was disappointed. There didn't seem to be even a trace of hurt in Miki's face, her voice. She was hiding it. Either that or the breakup wasn't as big a deal to her as Miranda thought. Miranda would have been grateful if Miki would simply belt her one or cry or scream — anything. It'd be so much easier if Miki hated her. Then maybe Miranda wouldn't have to beat herself up any more.

"Congratulations, by the way," Miki offered. "You

did great." She meant it; she just didn't feel much like smiling.

"Thanks," Miranda replied uneasily. She didn't know what to say, though so many things needed explaining, things Miki needed to understand.

Miki sighed and studied the early evening sky now breaking into streaks of orange and pink. She strained to remember that old saying about a pink evening sky, and how it meant a sunny day would follow. What was it? Something like, Red sky at night, sailor's delight . . .

Miki couldn't stand the silence any more. And at least she could try to set Miranda free, free of her own guilt more than anything else.

"Look, Miranda, don't beat yourself up. I know you've got things you want to accomplish, plans that don't include me." Miki turned to her, her face rigid. "I don't like it, but I know how you feel about your career and all. And besides, you never lied to me or led me on. You never said you loved me or anything like that."

The final words twisted painfully into Miranda just as Miki had intended. But that was as far as she dared to turn the knife. Though she felt the instinctive urge to hurt Miranda back, another part of her held off. She almost felt sorry for Miranda.

Miranda opened her mouth in a silent struggle for words. Miki would never know how painful it had been for Miranda to hurt her, and how she had hurt herself by keeping her heart at a safe distance.

A car horn interrupted Miranda's thoughts.

"That's them." Miki smiled and offered her hand one final time.

CHAPTER EIGHT

Miranda carefully slipped the diamond ring from her left hand and stashed it in the empty ashtray of her pickup truck. It would be safe there if anyone broke in.

She checked herself one last time in the rearview mirror before hopping out and slamming the door behind her.

The short walk to Lola's Club was a brisk one. It was a cool September night, almost too cool for her light windbreaker. The massive city had groaned and squawked its way from the bustling business activity of day to the brash festivity of a Friday night. People in small gatherings lingered on the sidewalks. Cars cruised past, music blasting, horns tooting in competition.

While Miranda enjoyed her twice-yearly forays to Toronto for its nightlife, she'd surprised herself by growing to savor the isolated, rural atmosphere of her small city two hundred miles north.

Taking a seat at the bar, Miranda ordered a beer and took in her surroundings. Lola's hadn't changed in the five months since her last trip — even some of the women's faces looked vaguely familiar. A few women sat in pairs at the booths along the wall, while other women crowded around the two pool tables. Another half-dozen were dancing to the strobe-synchronized Aretha Franklin sound track. Only two other women sat alone on bar stools, each separated by at least a couple of empty stools.

Miranda didn't go out of her way to acquaint herself with anyone. She preferred it that way. Not usually one for noisy bars, Miranda nevertheless found herself more at ease each time she visited Lola's. Just being in a large room full of lesbians like herself gave her a few hours of silent comfort and reassurance before the trek back to Hooperstown and life as the greatest imposter of all. She sipped from the glass of beer placed in front of her and thought of her return home. Dread pulled at her.

Miranda had no difficulty admitting to herself that she was a lesbian, although to what degree, she wasn't sure. Is anyone really one hundred percent straight or gay? Or are we a little more one than the other? she mused. But one thing she was sure of was that she had a choice. Just because she preferred women didn't mean she had to live her life loving women only. If others wanted to live exclusively as lesbians, well, bully for them. But for Miranda, it just didn't fit into her plans right now. And it probably never would.

She covertly sized up the two other single women at the bar — one, jean-jacketed and plump, seemed absorbed in her near-empty glass and smoldering cigarette; the other was slim and long legged in a tight denim skirt, long chestnut hair cascading over a low-cut, black silk shirt. *Hmmm, a real femme, and a good-looking one.* The woman settled penetrating brown eyes on Miranda, prompting Miranda to quickly glance away. Shit! She hated it when she did that.

It was habit for Miranda to do a physical take on any strangers. Invariably in any public place, she'd sit facing the door to watch people come and go. She'd memorize their clothing and faces for future reference. Her mind was like a giant filing cabinet with remnants of people's physical attributes tucked away to be called up at will. It could be the sound of their voice, the shape of their eyes, the way they walked. It came in handy when patrolling the beat or looking for a runaway teenager. And even though she didn't need to file away characteristics of people in a strange city, she played out the exercise anyway to be sure she didn't recognize anyone. She was especially careful to stay away from women at the bars who resembled cops. It would blow her careful cover to be recognized in a dyke bar.

Miranda sipped her beer, smiling as she watched a young lesbian couple dance closely to a love song. The taller one held the shorter one by the waist; the shorter one had wrapped her arms tightly around her lover's neck. They swayed as one to the sultry music, with their cozy whispering alternately turning to giggles.

Miranda was envious. She longed for that intimacy — the shared secrets, the private joking, the thrill of imminent sex. Her coworkers and acquaintances all thought she was the lucky one, in love with one of Hooperstown's most eligible bachelors. But only she knew the truth, the longing, of what wasn't. It was at times like this she wondered if she could really go through with this marriage thing. She hadn't felt true intimacy with anyone since Miki Paxton. *Oh, Jesus, Miki.* Miranda felt a tiny pinch of anger, that feeling of being cheated that she'd felt so often over the past three years. *Why couldn't you have been a man, dammit! It would have been so easy. I'd have married you in a flash!*

Miranda's breath left her for a couple of heartbeats. She felt nauseous, the way she always did when she thought of having rejected Miki for the sake of her career.

But what a career it had become in those three years and two months since police college graduation. Each year she racked up more charges and arrests than any of the other two dozen uniforms at work. And six months ago the city had given her a commendation for single-handedly subduing and arresting an armed robber as he fled a fast-food joint. She was sure she'd get the next promotion, if only she kept working hard and, equally important, kept doing all the right things.

Ken Cardwell was a big part of those "right

things." He'd accomplished so much for a thirty-year-old. He had a master's degree in business administration, was vice-president and general manager of the family's large auto-parts factory, and a member of all the right service clubs and volunteer groups in town.

Miranda frowned. Her chief was quite impressed with Kenny, as he called him, and even more impressed with Ken Sr., mayor of the city and the man who held the police department's purse strings. The Cardwell family's spell over Chief Burridge reached even further back. Ken's grandfather was the police chief who hired Burridge as a young cadet some thirty-odd years ago.

"Another beer?" The young woman behind the bar winked at her, sensing her sullen introspection. Miranda's broad shoulders slumped, heavy with the weight of the world's problems, or at least with her world's problems. The barkeep had seen plenty of women on her stools like that before.

"Yeah, sure." Miranda's smile was a poor attempt. She caught the eye of the leggy woman to her left as she answered. This time she held her stare a moment longer.

"Thanks." Miranda accepted the refilled glass and pulled a couple of bills from her jeans pocket.

She drifted back to the lusty hour she'd spent with Miki in the sauna at the police college — the first time they'd made love. God, how she'd burned and ached inside to feel Miki's hands, her tongue, all over her. The memory was as real as ever to Miranda. She often played it over and over in her mind, like a scratchy, favorite old 45, when she was out patrolling the streets alone at night.

Miranda drew in a deep breath and let the air out slowly, feeling suddenly warm and crowded in the bar. She hadn't made love with a woman since Miki, and still she thought of her each time she feigned orgasm with Ken. What would she do, she wondered now, if Miki suddenly walked through the door. After all, it was Miki's city. Maybe some of the women here even knew Miki. Or shit, even dated her. Her heart surged.

Miranda lifted her eyes from her glass and looked cautiously about. She felt so transparent, even vulnerable. Maybe she ought to leave. Maybe she shouldn't even come to places like this if all it did was remind her of what she would never have again.

"You look pretty lost in thought."

Miranda turned to the suddenly-occupied stool beside her. It was the leggy brown-eyed woman who slid her drink over as she talked.

"Don't tell me you had a fight with your girlfriend," she smiled inquisitively at Miranda.

A well-practiced opening line, no doubt. Miranda pursed her lips and looked into the woman's smoldering, dark eyes. It'd been so long since she'd made love to a woman — to Miki — and she felt the familiar arousal tickling her. Every other time she'd visited Toronto's women's bars, she'd pretty much kept to herself, too scared of losing her anonymity. But this might be her last chance before she settled into her scripted role as Mrs. Cardwell.

Miranda relaxed and held the woman's seductive stare. Maybe if she could make love to a woman once more it'd be enough. Or better yet, maybe she wouldn't even like it anymore. Perhaps Taylor and Miki had simply been curious distractions.

"What's your name?" Miranda braved, staring at naked breasts swelling beneath silk, taut nipples tantalizingly discernible.

"Maggie," she answered quickly. "And yours?"

"Alex," Miranda lied with surprising ease, her eyes drifting to the woman's sly smile.

Maggie's full red lips were parted to reveal perfectly rowed teeth. "Hmmm, I like that name." Her voice was deep and a little raspy, as though she'd smoked cigarettes all her life. "Short for Alexandria?"

"Alexis, actually," Miranda lied again, enjoying the game. Big cities did have their appeal — you could be anyone you wanted. There was no one to stop you in the mall or in a restaurant to ask you how to get out of a speeding ticket or how to go about dropping charges against an abusive partner.

"Don't think I've seen you here before," Maggie hinted. "In fact, I know I haven't. I would have remembered those eyes of yours."

Miranda smiled a little shyly. She was playing right into the seduction game this woman was obviously no stranger to. "I've only been here once before, months ago. I'm from out of town."

Maggie sipped her drink without taking her eyes off Miranda.

"Care to dance?" she asked, her drink nearly drained.

Miranda smiled into her glass, shaking her head coyly. "Not really, thanks."

Maggie's eyebrows shot up in surprise.

"It's just that I'm kind of feeling claustrophobic in here," Miranda answered, settling a long look on Maggie, whose eyes were like deep, dark pools that swallowed up her pupils. Her nose was rather long and fine-boned, but she had a strong chin and jaw line. Miranda's gaze slithered down to her nyloned knees. She had an urge to slip her hand under that tight skirt.

"Well, then," Maggie licked her lips. "I know a much quieter place. My apartment's only three blocks away."

Leaving her truck behind, Miranda walked the short distance with Maggie to her second-floor flat above a flower shop. Maggie was doing her best to find out more about "Alex." When her attempts met with vague answers, she fell into a dull explication of her own life as a twenty-nine-year-old blood technologist who still dreamed of a career in modeling.

Christ, don't people ever just go to bed with one other? Why the need to spell out your whole life story! Miranda tiredly trudged up the steps, already bored with the game. The only thing she wanted to know about this woman was the feeling of climbing up those long legs.

Once inside, Maggie bolted the door and shed her leather jacket and heels. Slipping out of her own running shoes and windbreaker, Miranda watched the slender Maggie float into the tiny kitchen and bend over to retrieve a half-filled bottle of wine from the refrigerator.

Miranda's eyes followed her slim waist down to the curve of her tight, round ass. The clinging denim skirt was true to every inviting curve.

She soon appeared with two filled goblets. Miranda sipped as music droned from the stereo speakers.

"Hope you like Melissa Etheridge," Maggie shrugged.

Miranda set her glass down and resolutely strode to Maggie. Firmly, she pulled Maggie's glass from her hand and set it on the nearby bookshelf. Without a word, she drew Maggie's face to her own and kissed her hard. Peeking at Maggie's eyes, Miranda saw no resistance; she roughly kissed her again. Her other hand slid up Maggie's long inner thigh and crept underneath her skirt until she felt a lacy garter belt. They stood, bodies tightly clasped together.

Maggie moaned softly, straining for breath. Finally she shook her head free as Miranda's hand continued to glide steadily up until it connected with silk panties.

"The bedroom's just in there," she whispered, soaking up the hunger in Miranda's eyes and returning it.

Miranda smirked and commandingly slipped her fingers between silk and skin. "I want you right here. Right now."

Miranda had never picked anyone up for spontaneous, no-strings sex. The freedom, the indulgence of it, exhilarated her. Her clitoris twitched in response, yearning for the touch of this woman.

Tugging Maggie down to the plush carpet, Miranda impatiently pulled the denim up with one hand and slid the silk panties down with the other. It'd been too long — far too long!

"Ohh," Maggie moaned, wet from Miranda's uncontrolled craving. Persistent fingers plunged inside Maggie as Miranda's mouth found its way to her breasts. There Miranda lingered, sucking and nibbling while her fingers danced inside Maggie's welcoming vagina. Seeing that Maggie was on the edge, Miranda trailed her tongue down her belly, finally sucking on her inner thigh. As the moaning grew, Miranda planted her mouth on Maggie's thrusting crotch, catching her wet mound at the peak of every lunge. She pushed hard with her mouth until Maggie erupted in orgasmic spasms beneath her. Miranda's tongue moved up to lick the light film of sweat forming in the crevice between Maggie's breasts, her thoughts turning now to her own need for sexual relief.

"Oh, Alex," she breathed, fingering Miranda's short brown hair. "You certainly aren't shy."

Miranda's eyes darted from Maggie's breasts to her face. Her hands grasped Maggie's narrow shoulders and gently but firmly rolled her on top of her. She wasn't in the mood for conversation.

Maggie kissed the tip of Miranda's nose. "Turn over."

Miranda's eyes questioned briefly before she obeyed and turned over on the floor. She felt Maggie's groping fingers undoing her jeans, then pulling them down. She lay perfectly still as her shirt was pushed up from behind, Maggie straddling her. Soft, full breasts swept across her back, pressing snugly against her.

Miranda imagined those soft breasts belonging to Miki as the tiny pointed nipples drew an abstract pattern. Gentle fingers crept under her from behind, finally settling on her engorged vulva. *Miki's fingers had felt like that . . .*

Miranda closed her eyes, letting expert fingers guide her to the brink while she visualized herself chasing a teasing, naked Miki. Finally at the precipice, Miranda dove over, never having quite captured Miki. Her orgasm was explosive, but it felt as though more were lurking below.

"Now how about that wine?" Maggie giggled in her ear.

Together they rose and reassembled themselves. Except for flushed faces, any signs of lovemaking had quickly been obliterated.

Funny how you can totally open your body to someone and in moments be strangers again, Miranda contemplated.

They sipped their wine.

"I don't even know your last name, Alex," Maggie tested.

"Does it really matter?" Miranda couldn't keep the bitterness from her voice. All she'd come here for was a good fuck. If she'd wanted conversation, the bar or a coffee shop would have done just fine.

Maggie shot a look of irritation at Miranda. "No, not if you don't want it to." She lit up a cigarette.

Miranda nodded, jaw set. "Look Maggie, I really should go. Thank you for the wine, and . . . well, thanks."

It was nearing midnight as Miranda made her way back to the darkened parking lot three blocks away. She heard some distant noises, but walking alone at night didn't bother her, even though she couldn't carry her gun off duty without all sorts of special permits and red tape. In fact, she enjoyed the quiet solitude of walking alone at night.

Shouting and cheering sounds grew louder with each step. As Miranda rounded a corner, she saw a crowd of about two dozen people gathered on the sidewalk outside a bar a few hundred yards away.

They were mostly shadows, but she could make out some pushing and shoving. The onlookers began circling as if watching a fight.

As Miranda slowed to keep an eye on the situation, a patrol car sped past, its flashing lights slicing the darkness. Tires squealed to a stop before the crowd. Pausing behind a light pole, Miranda watched the two cops, tonfa sticks in hand, emerge from the car.

The officer who had hopped out of the driver's side was a tall, stocky man. His partner, a smallish woman, appeared to be talking into her portable radio as she rounded the front of the car.

Miki? Miranda's mouth went dry. She couldn't tell for sure at this distance, but the way she carried herself . . . the way the fair hair appeared tucked in behind the cap . . . her wiry build.

A backup unit pulled in behind the first patrol car, and two more officers emerged and waded into the scattering crowd.

Miranda realized she was breathing quickly. Her head felt light. Pulling the collar of her jacket up to shield her face, she hastily stepped off the sidewalk and crossed the street to her truck.

Once inside, she sat in the darkened cab, frozen into place. Why did she feel like this every time she thought of Miki?

She berated herself. Why does this woman still hold a spell over you? You're weak, Miranda. You're mush. And this Maggie, what the hell are you doing fucking a total stranger? *Fucking a stranger and wanting Miki the whole time.*

Miranda let her head drop to the steering wheel. She felt like crying, or pounding her fist through something. But she swallowed her guilt instead and gripped the wheel. Crying would only remind her of the time Miki had held her, soothed her, sheltered her. That had been the last time she'd really cried. Not even at the car accidents, the sudden deaths. Only with Miki.

By the time she pulled out into the street, the patrol cars had disappeared into the night, the crowd having long gone.

CHAPTER NINE

When Miranda returned to Hooperstown, she immersed herself in her work. Even on her days off, she was at the office perfecting her paperwork or reading court transcripts to prepare for upcoming trials where she'd have to testify. She went to any lengths to avoid thinking of Miki or her one-night stand with Maggie.

At the same time, she avoided Ken. She couldn't be around him right now. Would he be able to see it in her face? Or hear it in her voice? She couldn't maintain the facade, not after reliving her past and having made love with a woman again.

Work excuses kept him at bay, though she couldn't put him off forever, she told herself as she absently steered the police cruiser down a narrow alley. *How long before Ken starts demanding answers, before he senses something's wrong?*

Maybe she could ease her way out of this relationship. If she could get out of it quietly and tactfully, maybe it wouldn't hurt her career. Single people were promotable too, as long as they came across as stable and weren't promiscuous. *Maybe if Ken got the idea that something's wrong, it wouldn't be so bad after all!*

Boxes and garbage bags were piled high outside the back doors of the row of downtown businesses. It was early yet. The dashboard's digital clock blinked seven forty-five. The storeowners hadn't arrived yet to get ready for another day's business. Miranda liked to start her twelve-hour day-shifts by cruising alleys behind the stores checking for open doors, broken windows, or any other signs of overnight break-ins.

She shook herself from her brooding, forcing her attention to the windows and doors. *Get with the game Miranda!*

Everything looked in order, even the sleeping, blanketed heap behind a large brown garbage bin she knew would be Max Detweiler, one of the city's homeless drunks.

Easing the large Caprice to a stop, Miranda got

out and stretched, taking her time. It was going to be another warm day. With luck, maybe Indian summer was here. Maybe she'd even get the chance to hit the golf course soon and whack her frustrations away. Filling her lungs with the garbage-tinged air, Miranda felt like smiling. A new sense of freedom, of hope, felt closer than it had in a while.

Squatting, Miranda tapped the blanketed mound. When it didn't stir, she firmly shook it.

"Max, hey wake up, Max!"

Finally a low groan emerged from deep inside the curled up, motionless heap.

Miranda shook her head at the sight of the empty bottle of cheap Scotch whisky lying beside him.

"C'mon Max, I haven't got all day. Wake up!"

Miranda rarely bothered the few homeless who roamed the streets and slept behind trash bins or under bridges unless someone — a taxpayer, that is — complained about them. But she knew Max was routinely up with the sun, and the fact that he wasn't worried her a little.

After another minute, a tousled gray mop and unshaven face poked out from the thinning, wool blanket. Squinting and blinking, Max tried to focus on the face and the uniform leaning over him.

"Yeah, yeah, whadya want?" he barked impatiently.

"It's late, Max. Don't you think you better get moving along? These stores will be opening soon."

Max sighed heavily and sat up, rubbing his eyes. "Okay, okay, I'm goin'. Now leave me alone."

Miranda smiled and stood, thumbs resting on her thick leather utility belt. She knew Max liked her because she was about the only cop in town who didn't routinely treat him like a nuisance. When winter came, she always made a trip to the Salvation Army to get a heavy coat for him. Grumpiness was just his way.

"All right, Max. Have a good day."

Getting back into the car, the radio crackled to life.

"Dispatch to Car Five."

Miranda retrieved the mike. "Car Five, go ahead."

"Ten-nineteen the station. Chief would like to see you."

"Ten-four."

The station house was just stirring to life. The brass and some of the office staff were just starting their day. The scent of fresh coffee wafted through the air, awakening Miranda's taste buds and reminding her that she hadn't had her morning coffee yet.

Miranda's knock on the chief's half-opened door induced a friendly invitation.

"Good morning, sir," Miranda smiled and shook the chief's outstretched hand. He clasped it warmly for an instant and settled a fatherly smile on her.

"Always good to see you, Miranda."

Miranda nodded and took the seat she was directed to. Instead of crossing back to his desk, Jackson Burridge took a chair beside Miranda's and repositioned its angle to face her.

"So, how is everything with you and Kenny?" he asked sincerely.

Miranda had always gotten along well with the

chief, not an easy feat considering his thinly-veiled opinion of female police officers. He didn't seem to think women were cut out for the dirty work on the streets, and he wasn't the only one on staff with that antiquated opinion. Miranda was one of only two female officers on staff, but she was the only one working regular street patrols. The other woman worked in community services, handling public relations, working with children — the kind of stuff Miranda disdained and where she felt female officers were too often pigeonholed.

But the chief quickly, if not reluctantly, had come to respect Miranda's ability, and her tireless work ethic helped boost the department's stats. She made the brass look as though they were at least shuffling into the twentieth century with respect to equal hiring. Burridge was amused by her intense ambition and dry sense of humor. And her engagement to Ken Cardwell Jr. was the icing on the cake as far as he was concerned. He seemed to take a fatherly pride in the matchup, partly because he had introduced them at the police banquet a year ago.

"Everything's just fine with Ken and me," Miranda answered with a strained smile, forcing herself to play the promotion game.

"Well, I'm glad to hear that. Business booming at the factory?"

"Working around the clock."

"Isn't that great! Bet that's keeping young Kenny busy."

Miranda hated it when he called him Kenny. She nodded absently, curious as to why the chief had called her in. He could drive a person crazy with his chitchat. It wasn't that he tried to be irritating; he simply felt everyone should adhere to his relaxed pace.

"Listen, Betty and I would love to have the two of you over for dinner next week. We haven't seen you two since you made the big announcement."

Miranda stalled, desperately searching her mind for a forgotten commitment, any excuse. But she knew he'd be persistent and keep asking if she put him off.

"Sure, that sounds great. Let me check with Ken's schedule."

"Of course," he gestured with a wave of his hand. Burridge raised his long, bony body from the chair and meandered over to his coffee brewer. He was obviously in no hurry.

"How about a cup of coffee with me, Miranda?"

Miranda settled back and stretched her long, athletic legs, resigning herself to the fact that he wasn't about to send her on her way any time soon. Setting up a dinner date couldn't be the only reason she was there. "Sure. Just a little cream please."

The chief returned with two steaming mugs and sat back down. Miranda sipped her coffee in silence as Burridge stroked his thin graying mustache and fixed his ice-blue eyes distantly at the ceiling.

"Miranda," he began, choosing his words carefully, "I don't suppose you've heard yet, since I was only informed yesterday, but Sergeant Fitzpatrick has submitted his retirement request."

Miranda instantly perked up, her senses keenly sharpening.

"It surprised me, too," Burridge said, reading her mind.

He reached his long arm out to his desk and

shook an untipped cigarillo free from a pack lying amid some paperwork. Fetching a lighter from his shirt pocket, he lit it, letting the smoke course to the ceiling in a small cloud.

The smell reminded Miranda of the ones Taylor Whiteside used to smoke. *Probably the same brand. God, what a millennium ago that was.*

"Anyway, he'll be leaving us in thirty days." Burridge slowly shook his head from side to side, gazing off to the ceiling again. "Don't know what he'll do. Probably drive his wife crazy."

Miranda waited, her impatience mounting. Her foot began tapping involuntarily.

"So we'll be short a sergeant. Do you know it's been five years since we've needed to promote someone to sergeant?"

"No, sir, I didn't realize that."

Burridge absently stared off again, alternately puffing with one hand and sipping from the mug in his other hand. "As you can appreciate, in a small department like this, and with just four sergeants, these things don't come along very often."

Miranda sipped from her own mug. "Yes, I realize that."

The chief returned his gaze to Miranda. "You know, Miranda, I like what you've been doing here since you joined us. You've worked twice as hard as any of the others, and it hasn't gone unnoticed."

"Thank you, sir," Miranda smiled modestly, not sure if he really meant it.

"Indeed, surprised the hell out of some around here," he chuckled.

Miranda chewed the inside of her cheek. *Surprised you too, by your tone.*

His coffee cup drained, Burridge placed the empty mug on his desk. "Care for a refill?"

"No, thank you, I'm fine."

"Very good, Miranda. Shouldn't overload on the coffee, you know. Betty's always getting after me about that."

Miranda cleared her throat impatiently, curious as to why he was telling her about the promotion in private. Curiosity kept her from excusing herself.

"Anyway, where was I? Oh yes, as I was saying before, I've been quite impressed with you, Miranda." He lowered his voice. "And just between you and me, I want you to seriously consider applying for this promotion once it's official. All the papers still have to go through yet, you know, so it'll probably be a couple of weeks."

Miranda was pleased, though a little surprised she was being sought out. She always figured she would have to fight tooth and nail just to prove to the brass that she should even be considered in the same league as the more senior men come promotion time.

Burridge beamed his fatherly smile at her. "I think you'd make a fine sergeant one day. But it won't be easy around here, you know, though I suppose they'd get used to it. They have to. It's the way things are going." He sighed. "What the government wants, the government gets."

Miranda wanted to roll her eyes. Even when he was trying not to be sexist, he just couldn't help himself.

"In fact, we're in the process of hiring another officer, I suppose you've heard?"

"Yes, sir, I'd heard that."

"Yep," Burridge exhaled smoke, his unblinking gaze shifting to the ceiling again. "Likely have to hire a woman. We're kind of low in that area, you know." Then he caught himself and shifted uncomfortably. "Well, yes, I guess you would know that."

This time Miranda did roll her eyes. Is that why he wanted her to apply for the promotion? Because the department has to hire and promote women? Or, god forbid, that her future father-in-law was using his influence with the chief? She squinted cynically. It didn't mean she'd get it, but having a woman in the running would make Burridge look good to the police commission and the government. By god though, she'd give it a damn good run. She wanted this, no matter what the hidden agenda was. And she'd make them look like fools if they passed her up.

"What do you think, Miranda?" he stared at her.

"Well, sir, I'm flattered. And I certainly won't deny that you've piqued my interest."

Burridge stood, Miranda following his cue. "I'm glad to hear that, Miranda. And I wish you luck."

"Thank you, sir."

"So, did you hear Fitzpatrick's retiring?"

Miranda turned to look at fellow officer Jeff Rowe, who had joined her in the police cruiser for the afternoon patrol. Much of the time the officers rode alone, but today there were too many bodies and not enough marked cars.

He stared ahead, smirking slightly, as he maneuvered the car around a tight corner.

Word travels fast, she thought wryly. Yet the chief had acted that morning like he was letting her in on a big secret and giving her some kind of head start. Maybe he'd done the same thing with Rowe.

"Yeah, I heard rumors about it," Miranda offered reluctantly. She wasn't about to be baited by her fellow constable, who no doubt had designs on the promotion himself.

Rowe had the advantage of experience over Miranda. He was thirty-three, married with a couple of young kids, and a university graduate like herself. He'd kept himself out of shit, though his record on the department didn't spell out any great accomplishments, either. Also working against Miranda was the fact that Rowe and her fiancé were friends — they played on the same baseball team and used to double-date. He'd probably weasel her plans out of Ken, who had no idea what competition was all about, being an only child and having his father's company handed to him lock, stock, and barrel. She'd have to be careful.

He cast a sideways glance at Miranda. "These promotions sure don't come up very often, you know. Everybody'll be throwing their hats into the ring."

"Yeah, I'm sure they will." Miranda feigned indifference.

The late afternoon traffic began to pick up as cars jockeyed for rare parking spots on the street and drivers made their way home from work. Prime time for accidents, Miranda thought as she checked the passenger-side mirror.

"Who do you think will try for it?"

Miranda yawned. "I dunno. Like you said, probably just about everybody."

"Yeah, well, I wouldn't mind it myself, you know. It'd sure make Joanne real happy."

He lowered his voice to a near whisper. "You know, Joanne and I, we've been having our problems. I think she's getting bored with things here. She'd love to move somewhere more exciting. But this promotion, you know, I mean if I got it, I think it'd go a long way to help things at home. And we could sure use the extra money, with the kids getting older and all. Though I guess you and Ken, well, money certainly wouldn't be a consideration for you."

Miranda glanced at the puppy-dog look in his eyes. It was obvious he had sized up Miranda as his toughest competitor and he wanted her to feel sorry for him — and more than that, guilty.

Miranda bristled. *How dare you pull that shit? Whatever happened to letting the best person win?*

Her anger slowly simmered to a low boil, and it was all she could do to control her temper. When she didn't answer, she could see his chin sink into a sulk.

"Well?" He couldn't contain himself any more. "Are you gonna try for it?"

Miranda exhaled loudly. "I don't know, Jeff. Fitzpatrick retiring was a surprise to me. I really haven't given it much thought."

He seemed satisfied with the lie. "You know

Miranda, it'd be an awfully big step, especially for someone like yourself still fairly fresh out of police college."

Condescending prick! Even if she hadn't been planning to enter the contest, she'd do it now anyway just to spite him.

Rowe was smiling like a Cheshire cat, but his tone was one of brotherly concern. "You really should think long and hard about it. If you were actually to get the promotion — and you could, you know, being a woman and all — you'd be in way over your head."

Seeing the sour look on Miranda's face, he desperately tried to backpeddle. "Hey, I just mean that some of the guys would give you a hard time, that's all."

Yeah sure, Miranda thought acidly. *Of course, you wouldn't be one of them, would you Jeff?*

"Look, Jeff, can we change the subject?"

"Sure," he smiled triumphantly as they passed a high school. Cheering students were gathered along the sidelines of a football field, and Miranda could see flashes of colored jerseys running across the field and the faint wave of cheers following.

"Hey," Rowe continued, "I heard they finished the last interviews this week for the new constable they're hiring."

"Boy, you're just a fountain of gossip today," Miranda interjected, her tone iced with sarcasm.

He ignored the remark. "I think the front-runner's a Toronto copper. Actually saw her at the station yesterday after her interview. Real looker, she was." He whistled.

"That's nice." Miranda was pissed off and bored and didn't care to hide it. *Phony asshole.* She resisted the urge to roll down the window and spit out the sourness gathering in her mouth.

"Can't remember her name though."

"Dispatch to Car Five. Can you take a call?" the radio interrupted.

"Ten-four," Rowe said into the mike.

"Attend nine-three-four Storey Street. See a Barbara Payton about a stolen motorcycle."

"Shit," he complained to Miranda as he wheeled the car around. "No decent calls these days. Just garbage stuff, ya know?"

Miranda sighed in agreement. "Yeah, it's been a while since anything exciting's happened around here. I suppose we're overdue."

Miranda enjoyed the thrill of a dangerous or stressful call. The adrenaline rush was like nothing else, except maybe a sudden death basketball game. But of course ball games weren't life and death.

The middle-aged woman met the two officers on her front porch. She was distraught and on the brink of tears.

"It's my Harley. It's just gone!" she gasped, raising a hand to her platinum head.

"A Harley, huh?" Rowe smirked.. "You ride a Harley, lady?"

Miranda shouldered her way past her coworker and introduced herself, all the while thinking what an imbecile he was.

"Can you show us where it was?" Miranda asked

helpfully, trying to make up for her partner's buffoonish behavior. She could appreciate the woman's attachment to her motorcycle. Miranda once owned a Honda Shadow 500 when she was at the university. She still toyed with the idea of getting another bike. *Yeah, maybe even a Harley,* she thought with a contemptuous smile as she looked at Rowe.

Miranda promised to pass the report on to one of the detectives and slid into the driver's seat.

Rowe flipped through his notebook, going over the notes he'd just taken. He scratched his chin. "Payton, Payton. You know, I think that was the name of that Toronto cop in for the interview yesterday. Or something like that . . ."

Miranda didn't hear him. She'd already retreated into thoughts of Ken, and how in the hell she was going to get out of the relationship and impending marriage. It was shitty timing now that a promotion was opening up. She felt herself wavering between doing what her heart beckoned her to do and using every advantage she could to get this promotion. She was afraid to rock the boat, especially since the chief was so fond of the Cardwells.

And yet, that night last weekend with Maggie had spurred all sorts of memories, memories she thought she'd buried for good since police college. The sexual intensity she'd felt hadn't been duplicated with Ken in the year she'd known him. *And it never will, not with a man.* She could see that now, just as plain as she could see the gun on her belt. There just wasn't that connection, that sense of being whole. How could she have second-guessed that?

She felt her heart sag at the memory of seeing Miki at that Toronto bar fight. If indeed it had been Miki.

Miranda stared absently ahead, more depressed than ever.

CHAPTER TEN

The ride to Jackson and Betty Burridge's house was torture. Silence was a normal part of any love relationship, but lately, Miranda's silences were troubled and frequent. There was something, Ken sensed, that she just couldn't, or wouldn't, talk about.

He struggled to start conversation, but Miranda simply grunted in acknowledgment. Ken felt Miranda steadily slipping away from him, like a lonely locomotive lumbering to life and picking up steam. It wasn't by accident. She was pulling away in a determined effort, he was sure, even if she didn't know it yet herself. But he refused to confront it head-on as he knew he should. He didn't want to lose her, not now, not after they'd told the whole world they were engaged. Such things weren't done in his circles. Confronting Miranda would surely lead to that; he felt it deep in his gut. Ken just hoped that whatever it was, it would pass quickly and she'd be her old self again.

"C'mon in, kids," Jackson Burridge beamed as he ushered them in. The Burridges didn't have any children of their own, and they habitually called younger people kids.

"It's so wonderful to see you," his wife echoed as she pressed filled wine glasses into their hands. "Come and sit down. We want to hear all about your big plans!"

Miranda stewed. She didn't want to discuss plans for a wedding that was never going to happen so far as she was concerned. She'd been stupid to ever agree to the marriage in the first place. She could kick herself now. Miranda McCauley didn't normally wither under pressure, yet she'd caved in with Ken. He and his family, the chief, everyone, wanted so badly for it to happen. Ken was so well liked in town, it was almost sickening at times. How could she say no to Mr. Perfect? Admittedly, she'd found herself attracted to his attraction for her, foolishly thinking it a substitute for some kind of love, even though it never compared to her fiery feelings for Miki.

Why does it always come back to Miki? Miranda stared at her folded hands in her lap. She couldn't deny the role her ambition had played in her present predicament. Getting engaged to someone like Ken could do wonders for her career profile in a rooted, religious community like Hooperstown. She'd sold out.

"Well?" Betty Burridge persisted.

"We haven't given the details much thought yet," Ken apologized after seeing that Miranda wasn't about to answer. He reached over and squeezed her hand. "But we hope to soon, don't we, honey?"

Miranda nodded and flashed her artificial smile. That eager look was in Ken's light brown eyes again. She knew he was eager to set some plans and to have something concrete to tell people before they began to gossip about what might be wrong. And they would. An engagement wasn't supposed to go on indefinitely.

"Surely you must have set a date by now?" Jackson asked skeptically.

Ken cleared his throat and glanced nervously at Miranda. "Well, I'd like to have the wedding as soon as possible." He winked at the older couple. "But you know women. Everything has to be just right."

Miranda stiffened. Christ, if she could just hold on until after the promotion, then maybe . . .

"Listen, Kenny." Jackson stood. "Come downstairs and see my new pool table. You girls can talk about weddings."

Ken shrugged at Miranda and followed the chief.

"Besides," he whispered, putting his arm around Ken's shoulder, "it's the only place Betty lets me smoke my cigars. So how's your dad?"

Miranda watched them disappear downstairs. Her chief seemed to treat Ken like a son. It'd probably break his heart — and her shot at the promotion — if she broke up with him now. Even though it was a panel of five, including the chief, that made the final decision, the chief's advice would carry a tremendous amount of weight.

She wrung her hands, feeling the sudden need to scream until her lungs burst. Christ! She felt so stifled! This town did that to people, even just after a short time. No one could walk a block without passing a church: big, cold, stony structures, their doors closed to outsiders. And people were considered outsiders if they weren't white, Protestant, and rooted to the land or the nearby lake through generations of tough, hard-living and less-forgiving folk. And the people lived up to the rigid molds cast by their forebears. But Miranda knew the other side of them, when they weren't in the fields or in the factories or in the churches. Like anywhere, there were the drinkers and the drug addicts, the abused and the abusers, the unforgiven. Because it was Miranda's job to clean up the broken hearts, the broken homes, and the just plain broken, she was tainted somehow. She'd seen what good people weren't supposed to see. She could never be one of them.

"Come into the kitchen with me, dear," Betty called out. "We can chat while I make the gravy. And I'll show you the wonderful cookbook I just picked up."

Miranda was glad when dinner was finally served. It meant they were that much closer to being able to leave, and she'd have a chance to mull things over some more.

Jackson plopped a large scoop of mashed potatoes

on his plate and passed the bowl along. "Listen, Miranda," his voice boomed as his hand shot up to signal a stop in his wife's direction, conceding her objection. "I know I shouldn't mix business with pleasure. But just today we officially hired our new constable."

"Oh?" Miranda feigned interest as she took a helping of mashed potatoes and doused the heap in gravy.

"As a matter of fact, I think you might know this officer. Graduated from police college about the same time you did."

"Really?" Miranda dipped her fork into the potatoes for a healthy bite. It could be anybody. There had been about a hundred fifty graduates in her class, and many of them she barely knew.

"She's been working for Toronto —"

She. Well that narrows it down to about fifty.

"— and I think she'll be a good one. Did real well in the interview, though I'm not exactly sure why she wants to come here. Probably just wanted to get away from the big city like —"

"Jackson, dear," Betty interrupted. "Why don't you just tell Miranda the woman's name. How else is she supposed to know if she remembers her or not?"

"Of course, of course. Sorry Miranda, I get a little sidetracked sometimes. Anyway, unusual name she has. Michaela Paxton. I think —"

The glob of potatoes caught in Miranda's throat. She began coughing and sputtering, hoping she'd misheard, hoping to god it wasn't the same Michaela Paxton, imploring the floor to swallow her up.

"Oh dear, are you all right, Miranda? She's choking, Jackson!"

Ken, who was sitting beside Miranda, began clapping her on the back. "Are you okay, honey? Just take it easy."

Miranda nodded, tears filling her eyes. She reached for her glass of water and washed the goo down; embarrassment took the goo's place.

Miki, coming here? Holy shit! It must be some kind of sick joke.

"I'm okay. Sorry about that," Miranda rasped, her wind and her composure coming back. But her face remained flushed.

"I think she goes by the name Miki," the chief continued after a moment. "Do you know her, Miranda?"

Stay calm, take your time. Just breathe. Breathe! That's it.

Miranda felt like vomiting. What she really wanted to do was excuse herself and go hide in the bathroom. But it wouldn't do for them to think something was wrong at the mention of Miki's name.

"Yes, yes I remember her," she muttered, trying to sound enthusiastic.

"Were you friends, dear?" Betty asked politely.

Miranda smiled, barely able to smother a giggle at the comedy of it all. If only these poor people knew! Oh, how'd they'd freak right out. It'd probably send them all scurrying off for the nearest church.

"You could say that." Her smile spread to a grin as she imagined the look of shock settling on their faces.

"That's good, dear. I'm glad to see you have fond

memories of her," Betty smiled. "Now, let's change the subject from work, shall we, you two?"

Miranda's shock over Miki's hiring soon began to give way to anger. What the hell was she up to, coming here to work? She knew Miranda wanted to work her way to the top with the Hooperstown police. And now her chances for promotion would hang in the balance. All Miki had to do was let a few hints drop about what had happened between them, and that'd be it. She could kiss Hooperstown and everything she had worked for good-bye, then start all over at the bottom somewhere else. Or perhaps all people had to do was see the way they looked at each other. One look might reveal their entire past!

After a few days of simmering resentment, Miranda noticed the memo for the promotion posted on the bulletin board in the station house's briefing room. There was a spot for officers to write their names, and a paragraph explaining they would be called for interviews over the next two weeks. A decision would be made soon after that.

Miranda bit her lip. It was now or never. She was twenty seven years old, and if she hoped to make chief before she was forty, it was time to start climbing the ladder now.

Miranda retrieved a pen from her breast pocket and added her name to the list. Sure enough, Jeff Rowe's name was one of the half dozen.

Miranda felt a mixture of relief and anxiety as

she looked at her signature. She was in now — there'd be no backing out, no matter what happened with Miki joining the force.

Miranda spun around, about to search for keys to a patrol car.

"Miranda," the soon-to-be-retired Sergeant Fitzpatrick growled in his usual cranky manner. "This is Constable Paxton."

Miki stood alongside the short, chubby sergeant, looking radiant in her perfectly pressed uniform, polished boots, and blond hair cut short now. She was incredibly cute. She held her hat with her right hand, a smile on her lips.

Gloating, is she?

Miki had hardly changed. She'd be thirty now, but her face looked as youthful as ever. She appeared to have put on a healthy five pounds or so. *God, you have no right to look so damned good!*

"Hello, Miki." Miranda extended her right hand as a bead of sweat trickled from her armpit down her side. Her tongue thickened, leaving her afraid of trying to string together more than a few words.

Miki flashed her perfect smile, tiny dimples on either cheek, and with just the right measure of politeness and firmness, shook Miranda's hand. "It's good to see you, Miranda." Her tone was warm but reserved, with just a hint of wariness. Her eyes revealed nothing.

"Guess you two know each other," Fitzpatrick mumbled. "PC Paxton will be joining our shift, at least until the end of the year."

After an awkward moment, he turned to Miki. "Jeff Rowe will be taking you with him to the courthouse today for security detail. He should be along any time." Fitzpatrick turned on his heel, clipboard in hand, and marched off to his desk.

Miranda forced a nervous smile. All week she had envisioned her temper boiling over upon seeing Miki again. She was counting on it. She wanted to chastise her for coming to her territory. But at the sight of her, Miranda surprisingly felt like a helpless little child. Her stomach cartwheeled, and she couldn't think of a damned thing to say.

"I, ah, I better get going," she finally managed.

Miki was secretly disappointed their meeting was about to end. She was hoping to get Miranda alone, in private, but it didn't seem to be in the cards today. Miki held her breath for a minute. *God, Miranda looks wonderful — strong, athletic, and her green eyes as intense and bright as ever. Though she does seem a little jittery.*

As Miranda turned to leave, Miki saw something flash under the fluorescent lighting. It wasn't anything on Miranda's black leather utility belt. Her portable radio was coated in black metal, her handcuffs and pepper spray had their own leather pouches, and her gun was made of dull gray metal with a wood handle. What was so shiny?

"Miranda," Miki burst forward, touching her lightly on the arm to stop her from leaving.

Miranda turned around, and it was then Miki saw it — a ring on her left hand — a diamond engagement ring! Miki's eyes widened. *What the hell is she up to? An engagement ring for chrissakes!*

"I, I'm looking forward to working with you," Miki stammered.

Miranda nodded coolly and strode off.

Miki was breathless. A heatwave rose from her

neck and settled in her suddenly throbbing temples. Curious, she sauntered over to the bulletin board where Miranda had been standing earlier.

OPENING AVAILABLE
Applications now being accepted for the position of sergeant upon Sgt. Gerald Fitzpatrick's retirement. Interviews will be conducted over the next two weeks, and a selection will be made by a panel of three shortly after. Please sign in the space below:

Miranda's name was eighth on the list.

CHAPTER ELEVEN

Miranda swallowed a dry gulp and hesitated. Heart thudding in her ears, she finally knocked.

After the fourth tap, Miki finally appeared, rubbing the sleep from her eyes. She tightened her hastily-fastened robe.

It was four in the afternoon, and both had worked the night before. But Miranda hadn't been able to sleep more than a couple of hours and had finally abandoned her sulking and intense pacing about. She could no longer tolerate the burning questions pushing her to an emotional precipice. Was

Miki here on some vengeful mission? To win her back? What?

Miki blinked in surprise when she saw Miranda through the screen door. In the week since they'd run into each other at the police station, Miranda had kept her distance. Now she was at her door, looking exposed and fearful, like a rabbit trapped in the beam of oncoming headlights.

"Come in," Miki offered skeptically, her stomach churning.

Miranda was awkward and uncharacteristically graceless as she scurried inside. *Probably afraid of being seen,* Miki thought bitterly.

"I was just about to put the coffee on," Miki finally uttered, trying to sound casual. She didn't want Miranda to guess the mix of concern and hope her appearance had produced.

Just play it cool, Miki reminded herself. She waited for a response from Miranda but got none. Miranda still hadn't said word one. Finally, Miki padded off to the kitchen and began spooning coffee into the filter, pretending not to notice that Miranda had quietly followed.

"Would you like to sit down?" Miki pointed toward the kitchen table as she flipped on the coffee maker. She felt stiff and formal, as if she were talking to the next-door neighbor instead of the woman she'd once tasted every inch of. It wasn't fair. How could you love someone so intimately, love every part of her physical and emotional being, then act like a total stranger? It was perverse. She felt betrayed.

Head down, Miranda paced the roomy kitchen.

Miki had lucked into renting the one-floor duplex

when she moved to Hooperstown. Miranda had sneaked a look in the personnel files at work for the address, but it had taken her days to gather the courage to confront Miki. It wasn't that she was afraid to demand answers to the questions tormenting her. That would be easy enough. The terrifying part was not knowing how she would act, how she would feel, alone with Miki for the first time in more than three years.

She shoved trembling hands in her pocket and watched Miki take a seat at the kitchen table. *God, how perfect she looks, even just having gotten out of bed.* Her eyes had that sleepy, pure look. Her fine, blond hair was tousled, reminding Miranda of the warm, sunny, passionate mornings they'd spent in bed together at the college dorm. Blushingly, she wondered if Miki was wearing anything underneath her satiny robe. She always used to sleep in the nude . . .

Miki sighed impatiently, daring to break the silence that had only been interrupted by the gurgling and burping of the coffee maker.

"Why did you come here, Miranda?" Miki prodded gently.

Damn her. She wasn't going to make this easy, Miranda frowned. But her courage was welling up now. She'd have to be strong here, take control. After all, it was Miki who'd come to her turf, trying to stir the pot. How dare Miki ask what she was doing here?

Miranda whirled around, her chest full, her face flushing crimson.

"What do you want from me!" erupted the words from behind clenched teeth. Hands flying out of her pockets, her fists unconsciously balled up. "What are you doing in my town?"

Miki was taken aback by the anger seething from her former lover. She'd been secretly fantasizing a happy reunion, a torch still being carried for her. She'd hoped upon seeing Miranda at her door that she'd had a change of heart, that she'd finally realized being with her was more important than a promotion and some phony engagement.

"I don't understand —" Miranda's fury numbed her.

"Don't play naive with me," Miranda cut in, the words spaced in an even cadence. "What the hell are you doing here? Are you trying to fuck with my life? Is that it?"

Miki stood and walked to the counter to retrieve two coffee mugs, summoning her composure. She refused to be drawn into the anger and to fuel Miranda's. If it was confrontation Miranda had come for, well, she would just have to leave without it.

Silently, Miki poured, sensing Miranda's frustration about to brim over again. Gingerly, she sprinkled a spoonful of sugar in each mug and slowly retrieved the cream from the refrigerator. Pouring methodically, she waited, letting the gathering clouds of Miranda's anger whirl about.

Miranda paced to the rhythmic clink of the spoon tapping against ceramic. Finally she stopped, arms defiantly folded over her chest. What she really wanted to do was take those fucking mugs from Miki and smash them against the wall. Maybe then she'd know she was serious, that she meant for Miki to get the hell out of her life.

Miki returned with both mugs to the kitchen

table and set Miranda's down in front of the empty chair. Taking her cup in both hands, Miki inhaled the steaming aroma and took a long, pleasing sip.

"You haven't answered my questions!" Miranda finally demanded, a little more resigned this time. Miki's apparent apathy and her usual air of control had tangibly deflated Miranda's rage. She sounded more whiny now than angry.

"We can talk about this civilly, you know." Miki pointed to the empty chair opposite her. "I've missed you, Miranda."

Miranda froze, blinking, totally unprepared for Miki's admission. She'd wanted a fight, an admission of guilt. She wanted a reason to hate Miki; it would make it that much easier to get on with her life.

Like a spanked child, Miranda slumped down. In a sure sign of retreat, she took her mug and sipped. The hot mixture warmed her stomach and calmed the turbulence inside.

"I just want to know why you're here," Miranda finally stammered, staring into her mug, afraid to look into Miki's eyes. *Damn you! Why do you always have to be in such fucking control!*

"What difference does it make why I'm here?"

Miranda didn't answer, but her visible torment spoke volumes.

Gently, Miki reached over and raised Miranda's chin until their eyes met.

"Miranda, you're tearing yourself apart inside, you know. I can see it all over your face." Miki wanted to smile. She knew now Miranda still loved her. If not, she wouldn't be full of rage one minute and so unsure of herself the next.

Miranda tried to look away, but Miki held her

chin firmly. She wished Miranda would be honest about her feelings. All those times she could never tell Miki she loved her, all the times she tried to shrink away from any sort of permanence, the running away to Hooperstown, and now . . .

"Miranda, why are you engaged?"

Miranda looked to the floor and said nothing. Her jaw was clenched, and Miki released her chin.

"You don't love him." It wasn't a question, and no answer was needed. Miranda's eyes told the truth.

Still, Miranda couldn't look at Miki. It was none of her damn business why she was engaged, or whether she loved Ken, the childishly rebellious voice in her head told her. But somehow, it *was* Miki's business.

"I know you don't love him the way you loved me, you know. You never told me, but I know you did." Miki's hand grasped Miranda's and held it tight, hoping all the love she felt for her would magically seep from her fingers into Miranda. "I saw it in the way you looked at me. I felt it in the way you touched me those times when you thought I was sleeping." Miki's voice had begun to quaver.

Miranda resolutely shook her hand from Miki's grip and stood.

She looked squarely at Miki and cleared her throat nervously. It was her last chance to make Miki believe she just wanted to be left alone. That she *had* to be.

"I'm happy with my life right now, Miki. Everything I've dreamed about is in my grasp now, and I'm not going to let it go."

Miranda turned to leave, her tough facade of lies threatening to shatter into a thousand pieces. But

Miki's hand firmly latched onto her elbow and pulled her back before she could make her escape.

"Did what we have mean so little to you?" Miki asked, incredulous. "How can you live with yourself?"

Miranda shook her head. To explain would be useless. "Tell me one thing," she said calmly. "Did you come here to try and get me back?"

"What difference would that make now?"

Miranda held her ground. "I need to know."

"All right, yes, that was a big part of my moving here. I had hoped you still felt something for me. Obviously I was wrong. You're so set on your precious goddamned career, you can't see anything else!"

Miranda's heart was in her throat. *Well, that's it.* She made a hasty retreat, allowing the screen door to slam shut behind her. *Maybe now Miki will leave me alone.* She climbed into her pickup, not daring to glance back to see if Miki was still watching. Her gut told her she was.

Miranda backed out of the driveway and onto the street. Shifting into gear, she felt her hand tremble. An undeniable sob rose through her chest. She couldn't drive more than two blocks before her tear-blurred vision forced her to pull over.

First Taylor Whiteside, and now Miki Paxton. With anyone else, her skin had always been as thick as steel. But with them, she'd lost herself and become an emotional midget. She hated herself this way. It left her feeling so alone, so out of control, so scared. No man had ever left her feeling so afraid of herself.

Miranda slapped the steering wheel. *Not this time, Miki. I won't allow you to do this to me!*

* * * * *

Miranda avoided thoughts of Miki and Ken and did everything she could to focus on her upcoming interview for the sergeant's promotion. If she could get through the promotion intact, then she could deal with her feelings.

Punishing the body was her answer. Lonely hours jogging or shooting hoops kept her .thoughts from holding her hostage. Keep the mind and body occupied and everything else would follow.

Autumn descended on Hooperstown and almost overnight trickled into the leaves, painting them bright gold or crimson red. Nights turned crisp and cold, where breath would swirl in clouds of white vapor.

Miranda could faintly smell burning leaves in the distance as she dribbled the basketball along the faded asphalt of the outdoor court. She closed her eyes and enjoyed the remembered sensation of diving into raked piles of fresh leaves. As a child, she was allowed to belly flop into the pile and recklessly roll around until she was layered in leaves. She smiled, the first time in days she'd allowed herself to do so. Surprisingly, it felt good. So did the layup she buried, and the twenty-foot jump shot after that.

"Thought I'd find you here."

Miranda stopped mid-dribble and turned around. Ken stood respectfully along the sideline, looking comically out of place with his trendy, dark sunglasses, double-breasted blue suit, and wine-colored tie. Every hair was combed perfectly in place. Nevertheless, Miranda thought he looked bored and rather defeated, his face pasty and sagging in the waning sunlight.

"Guess I'm too predictable," Miranda smiled as she approached him.

She kissed him lightly on the cheek, but she knew something wasn't right. He was stiff and unresponsive, and as he peeled his sunglasses off, his eyes looked as though he hadn't slept in days.

For the first time since she had agreed to marry Ken, shame swept through Miranda. Not for what she'd done to him so much, but for herself. She didn't even know herself anymore. Somewhere in all the deception and all the role-playing, she'd lost herself. Aside from the promotion, she couldn't even be sure what was important any more.

One look at him now told Miranda that her lies and her aloofness had taken their toll. He wasn't buying it any more. He was looking for a good dose of truth, and there was no choice but to give him some if they were to maintain any semblance of dignity.

It should have left her panicky, but instead she felt a strange pang of relief.

"Can we sit down?" Ken asked tiredly.

"Yes, let's."

The wood bench looked as battle scarred as Ken's face. Its finish was long faded and chipped, with various names and initials etching out their territory.

"You've been out here a lot lately," Ken said quietly, almost reflectively, as Miranda sat down beside him. "Something's on your mind, isn't it?"

Miranda hugged the basketball to her chest. She'd always taken refuge in the game when something was bothering her.

"I've been a little stressed out lately. Well, I guess more than just a little."

"It's not just the promotion, is it?" There was fear in Ken's eyes as he struggled with wanting to know the truth yet wanting to be protected from it.

Miranda didn't answer for a moment. She had to choose her words carefully, even though she didn't expect him to understand. Absently, she rubbed the ball, feeling the rough, nylon pores beneath her palm. The friction warmed her hand.

"This promotion thing has really sapped me," she stalled, evading the real issue the way she did so well. "You know how much I want this . . ."

"But you've been so distant with me lately. You've been shutting me out." Gently, Ken took the ball from her and let it drop to the ground. Then he took her hands in his. "Every time I try to make love to you, or show you any affection, you shut me out. That can't be just the promotion. It's me, isn't it? You don't want me any more."

He was right, of course. She had been avoiding him since her abrupt tryst with Maggie: Maggie's soft, smooth skin against her own, full breasts tickling her back, fingers dancing inside her. How could she possibly think of making love to Ken again — to any man — and the emptiness for her that went with it?

Miranda grasped Ken's hands tightly. "It isn't you, Ken, it's me."

"I don't understand . . ."

Miranda drew in a deep breath and let it fill her

cheeks before slowly exhaling. "I don't think I'm ready for marriage."

"What do you mean? You're twenty seven, you've got a good career, which you know I support, and you live in a nice town. What more do you want?"

"I know all that, Ken. I know that at this stage in your life you're supposed to get married. But it's not me."

Telling him the truth was harder than she could imagine. How could she tell him that women excited and charged her, not men. That women challenged and nurtured her spirit, not men. That women were worth living for and even dying for if need be. How could he possibly understand that all her soul and body craved for could truly only be met by a woman. And if he couldn't understand, surely it was ludicrous to think her bosses, her coworkers, and the whole town for that matter would understand. She felt defeated before she'd even begun.

Ken buried his face in her chest and began sobbing. Embarrassed, she pressed his head against her to shield him.

"I don't want to lose you, Miranda," he sobbed.

"But you deserve someone who wants what you want."

Miranda knew she should feel sorry for him, and she did. She was sorry that she'd led him on. But she felt even more sorry for herself. She was miserable that Miki Paxton could still stir her soul. And worse, that she had to deny that little glow deep in her belly that Miki ignited. The churning in her stomach, the trembling of her body, the sweaty palms, the quickened heartbeat, the sexy dreams that possessed her sleep — the sight or thought of Miki spawned all of those things, and it left her anguished. To act on those feelings would kill the career she had dreamed of and worked toward for years. And when thoughts of Miki reluctantly receded, she pictured herself in a white shirt with gold brocade epaulets, sitting behind a large desk and directing hundreds of other police officers.

Ken finally pulled his tear-soaked face away. "Look, honey, you can have all the time you want. We don't have to get married," he pleaded. "We can live together, or keep dating. Whatever you want."

"What I want, Ken, is some time to think about things, about us. I need some time on my own. And once this promotion thing is over, we can talk. Okay?"

Ken nodded, eager for any strand of hope to latch onto.

Miranda tugged the diamond ring from her finger and handed it to Ken. "I think you should keep this for now."

CHAPTER TWELVE

Miranda shifted in her chair, confidently resting her elbows on the polished conference table.

She was beginning to tire. Already the interview was dragging into its second hour, but she didn't dare exhibit any signs of the nervousness or emotional exhaustion aching within.

Miranda was the picture of professionalism and confidence in her dress uniform. Polished silver buttons gleamed beneath fluorescent lights. A narrow, white lanyard hung sharply from the left shoulder of her dark dress tunic. Matching it were crisp white gloves. Her uniform pants were creased to a fine edge, and she could see her reflection in her boots. Her hat, with its glossy brim and red band, rested on the lacquered table before her.

The first hour had been spent reviewing her credentials and the excellent results of her recent promotional exams. Next, the chief, the deputy chief, and the police commission board chair had quizzed her on legal points and police procedure. Then the interview swung to questions on management and policing theory.

"Now, Constable McCauley, as supervisor of five other officers on your shift, how would you ensure the respect of your subordinates?" asked Deputy Chief Ron Fairborn stiffly. His strained attempt at formality was more for the benefit of Board Chair Jane Fulsome than it was for her, Miranda guessed.

"First, I would see that the work was distributed as fairly and evenly as possible, and that would include myself taking my fair share alongside the others," Miranda answered without hesitation. "And by giving clear and direct orders, making decisions as quickly as the situation calls for, and by not acceding to the manipulation of others."

Fairborn curtly nodded in reply, a little unbalanced by Miranda's snappy retort. The girl could certainly think on her feet.

Miranda thought she glimpsed a small smile of triumph on Jane Fulsome's lips. Having the head of the board in her corner would certainly help when it came time to choose, Miranda figured. If the old boys were left to their own devices, they'd surely pick the worst possible candidate.

"What is your theory of what constitutes a good

manager?" Jane smiled with serious gray eyes, sitting back in her chair, a sheaf of papers in her hand. Jane Fulsome was the type to hold her cards fairly close to her chest, waiting, like a cool gambler, for just the right moment, knowing that moment would come, and it would be hers.

"A good manager is one who, foremost, treats people fairly and equally. One who must make clear and informed decisions, yet not be so arrogant as to not consider someone else's suggestions." Miranda paused long enough to show that her answers weren't rehearsed, though not hard to come by either. "A good manager must be seen as one who listens and is considerate of others' concerns or problems, yet isn't afraid to mete out discipline or make unpopular decisions."

That hint of a smile was on Jane's lips again. She was a hotshot lawyer in town, and her chest puffed up as though her prize witness had just scored a point with the jury.

"Do you think you'd have a problem getting men to respect you as their sergeant? Especially some of the more senior men?" Burridge cut in. He leaned forward, half expecting Miranda to fall on her face with that one.

Miranda smiled faintly, savoring what was to come. "Behind my back, people will say what they want to say. But as their sergeant, they either do as I direct them or I charge them under the Police Act for insubordination." She loosened her grip on the table's edge, feeling triumphant. "But I don't expect a need for that. There's no reason why we can't all act like the professionals we are."

Both men in the room shifted uncomfortably, and

Miranda knew she'd scored a few points, even if those points were begrudged. If they thought she was being a ball-breaker, well that was just too bad. They'd have to take her or leave her just the way she was.

The deputy chief cleared his throat. "How do you feel about the personal conduct of officers outside of work? Do you think the way people perceive you as a person is important?"

"Absolutely, sir. The public puts a lot of trust in us, and I think for our credibility to remain intact, we have to conduct ourselves impeccably."

"Well, you certainly have," the chief nodded.

Miranda smiled. They had nothing on her, not an ounce of dirt, and she'd make damned sure they never did. Miki had too much class to screw things up for her. Clearly, Miki had come to Hooperstown hoping to win Miranda back, and she was undoubtedly smart enough to know that revenge was the worst way to lure her back.

The three whispered for a moment before Chief Burridge stood. "Well, I think we have all that we need. We'll be making our decision in the next couple of weeks, and then we'll make our recommendation to the full board."

Miranda stood and, clasping her hat, walked to the end of the table to shake hands with everyone. "I appreciate the consideration."

Jane Fulsome stood too. Her short, thick silver hair made it difficult to guess her age, though Miranda figured her to be in her mid-forties. Her handshake was firm, and she, too, seemed to be sizing up the woman before her.

* * * * *

The night was so still, the purring engine of the patrol car was the only sound. Cars stood mute guard in front of darkened homes. Only the occasional blue shimmering from a television set flickered from behind thinly-curtained windows.

Miki sat silently in the passenger seat, periodically gazing about, looking for anything out of the ordinary. Sergeant Fitzpatrick had assigned them to partner up for the night shift, and neither had been able to come up with a viable excuse to avoid it.

The silence disturbed Miranda. She hated being at odds with someone she had cared for so deeply — and undeniably still did. But if they were to pick up from their last conversation, it would surely just lead to battle. Nor was she in the mood for another lecture from the stoic Miki about how she was deceiving herself and everyone else, and how this promotion just wasn't worth sacrificing happiness for, blah, blah, blah. Well, it was fine for Miki to live her life the way she wanted. She didn't give a shit about rising above the rank of constable. And she only stumbled across the idea of being a cop anyway. It wasn't a lifelong dream for her.

Miki chewed on her upper lip, sulking. Lately, she couldn't be near Miranda or even think about her without filling with rage. Miranda rejecting her was one thing. But getting engaged? What the hell was that nonsense about? It's the nineties, for chrissakes! No one needs to get engaged or married if she doesn't want to. And Miranda couldn't possibly want to. Miki could see it in her eyes. She could feel it in the way Miranda had hesitated when she had challenged her on it. Hell, any woman who'd shown the passion for her in bed that Miranda had couldn't want to marry a man. It didn't make sense.

Miki had casually asked around and heard nothing but praise for Ken Cardwell. Though she'd never met him, she often tried to picture them together in her mind. She just couldn't piece it together. Maybe it was just her ego talking, but Miki couldn't imagine Miranda needing anyone but her.

She bit harder into her lip, hoping the pain would distract her from her rage, this inner ache at the thought of someone else — anyone but her — touching Miranda, making love to her, holding her.

Engulfed in their own thoughts, both had pretty much given up on the idea of making conversation when the two-way radio interrupted.

"Dispatch to Car Three."

Miranda picked up the mike. "Car Three, go ahead."

"Attend a domestic disturbance at one-one-eight Bricker Street."

The address was all too familiar. Miranda sighed and wheeled the car left at the next intersection.

"Ten-four." Miranda replaced the mike in its holder, shaking her head. "What a surprise," came the mumble.

Miki looked at her. "Regular customers?"

Miranda nodded. "Henry and Shirley Wright. About twice a week they get roaring drunk and beat each other up. Either she calls us or the neighbors do, and by the time we get there, she wants us to go away."

Miranda sped through the empty streets, not bothering to activate the lights or siren.

"You mean she never wants to press charges?"

"Nope. Except one time she did, but before it even got to court, she begged the Crown Attorney to drop it. Says she can't live with him and she can't live without him."

Miranda was pleased she and Miki were communicating, even if it was just work related.

"So why don't you just charge him anyway?" Miki asked.

"Because he's usually as beat up as her. You'd have to charge them both, which I'm tempted to do one of these times."

Miranda parked the patrol car along the curb in front of the modest bungalow. She picked up the mike.

"Car Three is ten-seven at one-one-eight Bricker."

Grabbing her steel baton, she got out of the car. As Miki followed her up the walkway, they heard the smashing of glass from somewhere inside.

Miranda ignored the steps and hopped up on the porch, knocking loudly on the door.

"Open up, Mrs. Wright! It's Constable McCauley, city police."

Miranda waited for a minute and was just about to barge in when the door opened part way.

A fiftyish woman with long graying hair peeked from behind the door. Her face was fleshy and, other than her hair looking straggly and out of place, she looked fine.

"Can we come in, Mrs. Wright?".

"Why do you want to do that?" The woman was obviously miffed.

"Because we got a call, that's why."

"Everything's fine, you can just leave now. I shouldn't have called. It was a mistake."

Miranda placed the tip of her black baton against the door and clenched her jaw. "Either you let us in or we help ourselves in."

Reluctantly, the woman stepped back.

Miranda pushed her way past, Miki a step behind her. From the tiny foyer, they could see into the living room. The place was covered in old newspapers, dirty dishes, and an inordinate amount of bric-a-brac — the kind of junk people usually sold at garage sales.

"This is Constable Paxton," Miranda snapped as she crooked a thumb in Miki's direction. "Where's your husband, Mrs. Wright?"

"Kitchen, I guess."

Miranda followed the familiar narrow hallway until she came to the kitchen. Henry, a heavyset, balding man, sat at the table. He hoisted his heavy legs and planted his bare feet on the tabletop, his arms stubbornly folded across his chest.

"Whadya want?" he snarled, his left eye red and puffy.

Miranda glanced around the kitchen. Broken dishes littered the floor, obvious remnants of a throwing contest. The cool night breeze wafted through what had once had been a glass window, below it a half-empty bottle of whiskey.

"Having a problem with your window?" Miranda asked benignly.

"No problem," Henry growled. "I was a little warm, okay?"

"I understand you're not getting along tonight. Is that right?" Miranda looked to Shirley Wright for confirmation. But the woman simply turned her head. Henry shrugged.

"Would you care for a ride to the women's shelter?" Miranda asked Shirley. "They'll put you up for a while."

She shook her head and bore a caustic stare through Miranda. "I don't need nothin'. Why don't you just leave!"

Miranda ground her teeth and shot a quick glance at Miki, who stood at her right, about a half step behind. Since Miranda had been driving, it was her call, and Miki was simply there to offer assistance.

"Fine, we're gone. But just one thing." Miranda stepped up to the table, her patience as worn as their faces. Leaning in, she spread her hands, the baton still firmly clenched in her left fist.

"I don't want another call here tonight, you got that?" She looked to both of them, her eyes metamorphosing to deep jade. "Because if I have to come back here, I'm taking you both in, and you can share adjoining cells."

Miranda let her threat sink in, then turned on her heel. "Better get that window fixed," she shouted over her shoulder.

Miki shook her head as they got back into the patrol car. "Think they can get through the night in peace?"

Miranda smiled as she turned the key in the ignition. "What do you want to wager?"

"Five bucks says we'll be back!"

"Well, you can kiss five bucks good-bye. I'm telling you, Miki. Twice a week. They'll be good now until the weekend. But just to give you a break, let's say it's gotta be for the rest of tonight and tomorrow night's shift."

Miranda picked up the handheld mike. "Car Three to dispatch."

"Go ahead, Three."

"Things have settled down here. I don't think there'll be a problem here again tonight," she winked at Miki confidently.

Pulling the car out onto the street, Miranda looked back to see the lights clicked off inside the Wrights' home.

"Hey, Mik."

"Yeah?"

"Tell me something. When you used to skate, did you really have to wear those frilly little outfits like you see on TV?"

Miki's warm laugh washed over Miranda. "Yeah, and they even had sequins!"

Miranda threw her head back and laughed with equal zeal. "Hah! It's you, it's you!."

It felt good to laugh with Miki again. Miranda's heart felt about ten pounds lighter.

CHAPTER THIRTEEN

Weariness soaked into Miranda. She tried to massage it from her temples with one hand while guiding the steering wheel with the other. Working consecutive twelve-hour night shifts left her feeling like a wet dishrag.

She craved a cup of coffee as her patrol car snaked through the deserted streets, her mind drifting. She was riding alone tonight, which was usually just fine with her. But things had gone pretty well with Miki last night, and she found herself wishing they were riding together again. Maybe there was a chance they could actually be friends. At the very least, she hoped Miki didn't hate her.

"Dispatch to Car Five," Miranda heard over the radio. That was Miki's car.

"Car Five, go ahead," came Miki's voice. She sounded tired, too.

"Attend one-one-eight Bricker Street for a domestic disturbance."

Miranda chuckled. So old Miki would win the bet after all. She picked up her mike, knowing Miki was also alone. It was never a good idea for an officer to respond to a domestic alone, because things could heat up quickly before backup had a chance to get there. And two officers could separate the two combatants and calm them down.

"Car Three to Car Five," she cut in.

"Go ahead Three," Miki answered.

"I'll back you up. My ETA's about five minutes."

"Ten-four. I'm just about there."

Miki pulled up in front of the Wrights' home. Grabbing her baton, she remembered the bet she'd made with Miranda. She smiled, thinking of the crow Miranda would have to eat now. Or maybe she'd just make her eat the five bucks instead!

Miki started up the sidewalk toward the darkened house. Surprisingly, it was eerily quiet. Maybe the Wrights had settled down and gone to bed for the night. She knew procedure dictated she should wait for Miranda, but the couple had seemed harmless enough last night. Besides, it sure didn't sound or look like any fight was going on.

Miki knocked on the door and shouted out her identification.

After a couple of minutes Mrs. Wright answered the door, her face hidden in the shadows.

"We've had a call about a disturbance here, Mrs. Wright. Can I come in?"

The woman didn't answer.

"C'mon in, Officer Paxton," came Henry's voice from behind the door. He sounded overly friendly, almost jovial, as if he were inviting her in for a party. "And shut the door behind you."

Miki stepped in, still wondering why the house was shrouded in darkness. As she turned to shut the door behind her, something cold and hard brushed her head, something metallic. Then came the unmistakable, sickening sound of a shotgun shell being cocked into place.

"Drop your stick and put your hands up. Now! And don't turn around 'til I tell you."

Miki still hadn't seen Henry Wright's face, but his voice was full of deadly, misdirected rage. The blood drained from her face and settled in her stomach. She had to rein in her weakening bladder.

Her baton hit the floor with a dull thud as she threw her hands into the air. Miki closed her eyes, afraid to look, afraid to confront her own sloppiness and ineptitude.

Why did you turn your back to him to shut the door, you stupid ass! And not waiting for backup! Shit! You've really done it now!

Miki felt her gun being snatched from her holster, the barrel of the shotgun still at her head. Okay, okay, you got me, she wanted to scream. I fucked up. Now can we just call the game off?

C'mon Miki, think, think.

"Now turn around real slow," Henry Wright commanded, jamming Miki's service revolver behind his belt. He stepped back as she turned to face him, the gun leveled at her chest.

"Get back into the living room," he barked at his wife without looking at her. She was standing somewhere behind him in the dark. She quickly retreated as she was told. "And you," he spat at Miki. Sweat trickled down his chubby face, and his liquor-soaked breath stung her nostrils. "You make me sick. Get in there. C'mon, c'mon, we haven't got all goddamn day."

"All right, take it easy now," Miki breathed.

She stumbled along in the darkness, Henry following her.

"On the floor."

Miki dropped down next to Shirley, who was also sitting on the filthy carpet. The outside streetlight cast a pale white glow inside the room, and Miki could see the woman had a shiner and a bloody gash on her forehead.

"No, no. Lie down. On your stomach." A swift kick from him rolled her into place.

She swore to herself and bit her lip to stifle the searing pain in her thigh. The taste of panic was bitter in her mouth. He roughly pulled her handcuffs from her pouch and cuffed her hands behind her back, and she knew there was no way out. This was no game. The man was a drunken nutcase who was beyond the edge. She desperately searched her mind for some remnant of advice from police college or a long-forgotten textbook. What was she to do now?

"Don't even think about moving! What the fuck

are you looking at, bitch!" he yelled to his wife. He was panting with rage.

He stepped menacingly toward his wife before something outside caught his attention. The sound of a car door slamming shut stopped him in his tracks.

"Another fucking cop! You guys just don't know when to quit."

Miranda! Suddenly Miki's stomach twisted in agony at the thought of her unsuspecting colleague walking up to the house. She winced, sweat beading down her left temple. *Oh Christ, Miranda, please, get back to your car.*

Henry raised the gun to his shoulder. "Why, it's your buddy! The one who thought she was so tough last night." An evil chuckle escaped him. "Let's see how tough she is when this bullet takes her head off."

With every ounce of energy she could summon, Miki heaved her body into his thick legs just as the explosion erupted from the gun and sent glass shattering over them. She had no idea if her maneuver worked, but prayed it did.

As the gunshot reverberated across the neighborhood, Miranda spontaneously dove to the ground.

"Holy fuck!" she whispered to the cold earth, her cheek pressed against the damp grass. Her mind raced in tandem with her pounding heart. The voice in her head rambled as her mind tried to process what had happened. He's gone nuts, he really has this time! Why the hell did he have to pick now, on my shift, for chrissakes, on Mik — *Oh no, Miki!* Sure enough, Miki's car was dark and empty.

Instantly her senses ripened and her thoughts began to sharpen. Deftly, she slithered the short distance back to her car. She couldn't see anything in the darkened house, but it was obvious Miki was inside.

Miranda's heart jackhammered her chest as she crawled into the car. Was Miki dead? Or bleeding to death? And if she was alive — *oh God, please let her be alive!* — what was she thinking about? Was she scared?

Miranda squeezed her eyes shut to wrench the thoughts from her mind. There was no time to waste. Miki's life was at stake, and keeping her head clear might keep them both alive.

"Car Three. Gunshot fired. Officers need assistance," she panted into the mike, reminding herself to stay calm, if that was at all possible. Nothing at police college had prepared her for this moment. "PC Paxton is being held hostage at one-one-eight Bricker."

"Ten-four, Car Three. Backup's on the way."

"Request tactical unit and advise me of their ETA."

Miranda knew the tactical rescue unit would be a while because it was based more than a hundred miles away. It consisted of a group of heavily armed police officers specifically trained to rescue hostages or act as sharpshooters. The Hooperstown force was too small to have its own tactical unit, so it depended on one of a handful of units stationed across the province.

Miranda retrieved the shotgun from beneath the front seat and crawled out of the car. Crouching behind the cruiser's opened door, she listened intently. There was no sound but the rushing in her ears. Her hand quivered as she cocked a live round into the chamber.

"Henry Wright!" she yelled out, her voice echoing across the darkened neighborhood. Lights began flicking on as people peered out their windows to see what the commotion was all about. "C'mon, Henry, I know you're in there."

Miranda waited, afraid to breathe. She desperately strained to hear anything at all. But there was just dead silence.

All right, asshole.

Miranda reached inside the car. With the flick of a switch on the console, she activated the spotlight on the roof's multicolored light bar. Illuminating the front of the house, she saw the gaping hole in the front window where the bullet had penetrated. *So that's where they are!*

"Shut that fucking thing off," Henry finally growled from inside.

Miranda thought she saw a flash of clothing emerge from behind the curtain.

"Shut it off or your friend here buys it."

Miranda flicked it off, content in getting a response and knowing where he was holed up. And at least now she knew Miki was still alive.

"C'mon, Henry, drop your gun out that window. Come out of there with your hands up and we'll forget this whole thing before you get yourself in deep shit." She did her best to sound calm, authoritative.

"I ain't goin' nowhere. I'm sick of you fuckin'

pigs always coming to my house and telling me how to live. I'm about as sick of you as this piece of shit I'm married to."

"What do you want, Henry?" Miranda coolly persisted.

"Just get outta here!"

"All right, fine. Just let your wife and the police officer go, and we'll leave."

"Yeah, right! They leave and you'll shoot the place up! You got fifteen minutes to get the hell out of here or I start shooting. And your partner gets it first."

From the corner of her eye, Miranda caught sight of two other cruisers pulling up at the ends of the street, one to the east and one to the west. At least they had the good sense to stay well back.

"All units," came the dispatcher's voice on the radio. "Tactical unit's ETA is ninety minutes."

Miranda let her head drop against the car door. Ninety minutes was forever! This guy was corked, and Miki might not have that long. She might not even make it through the next fifteen minutes if he kept his word. If he was suicidal, he wouldn't care who died with him.

Oh, God, Jesus, no!

The thought of what might happen to Miki hit her in the stomach as hard as the hardest punch anyone could throw. All the air had been sucked out of her. If only she'd taken last night's call more seriously! And making a lousy bet over it! How could she have been so stupid, so cocky, thinking she knew these people inside and out? It was her fault Miki was in there now, a gun probably pointed at her

164

head. If only she'd radioed to Miki to wait for her. If only . . .

"Jesus, Miranda," Jeff Rowe gasped as he ducked into place beside her. He'd jogged through backyards to sneak into position. "I didn't know this guy was a gun freak."

"That makes all of us. Listen, where's Fitzpatrick?"

"He's at one end evacuating the neighborhood, and Neely's at the other. Guess we better dig in and wait for the experts, huh?"

Miranda looked at her watch. "Wright said he'll kill them within fifteen — well, about thirteen — minutes unless we leave."

Jeff Rowe's eyes widened. "Holy shit. You don't think he means it, do you?"

"Here, take my shotgun. I'm going to cover the back of the house. And I'll be radio silent."

"Don't do anything stupid, okay? Remember the rules."

Miranda shut off the volume control on her portable two-way radio and retreated across the road. Jogging behind a few houses, she went a half block before she cut across the street and behind the houses on the Wrights' side. At least the darkness was an ally.

Creeping softly along, Miranda suddenly remembered the broken kitchen window at the back of the house from the night before. With luck, maybe it was still broken.

C'mon, Miranda, you know the rules. Remember the exercise at the college and what they told you? Wait for the experts!

Miranda slapped the hard ground with her fist in frustration as she knelt behind a shrub. She could see the back of the house, but she couldn't make out from this distance if the kitchen window was still broken. Damp spots formed on the knees of her dark wool pants.

She stared at the darkened house and gritted her teeth, her eyes unblinking. *If he does anything to Miki, I'll kill the bastard!*

A sob began to swell in Miranda's chest, and her breath caught. The thought of finding Miki dead was more than she could bear — Miki, who'd only become a cop because she wanted to help people, and who'd only come to Hooperstown chasing Miranda's heart. Hell, she'd gone up to the house alone, probably laughing to herself about winning the bet they'd made.

Miranda buried her face in her hands and let the tears silently drip through her fingertips and onto the dew-coated grass. She could see Miki's face now, smiling in the sunlight as she lay on a blanket on the sand dunes. A steel vise was crushing Miranda's chest as her very soul gushed out onto her drenched hands.

Please God, don't let her die. I'll do anything if you just make this right. You can have my badge, I don't care. To hell with it all.

She glanced at her watch. There were only eight minutes left before Henry Wright might make good on his threat.

C'mon, get it together, Miranda, before it's too late. She needs you!

Miranda squeezed her eyes shut for a moment, feeling the moisture stick in her eyelashes. Then she plucked her .38 revolver from its holster. Gripping it tightly, she sprinted to a tree just a few yards from the Wrights' kitchen.

She exhaled in relief when she saw that the window was still broken. She could make out curtains fluttering in the darkness.

Ignoring the inner voice that warned against it, Miranda ran to the house and crouched beneath the window. The sound of her beating heart rushed in her ears and drowned the silence.

Miranda slowly stood and with one eye, peeked through the window. Though it was dark, she could see no movement or unusual shadows. It looked clear, and it was her only chance.

Reholstering her gun, Miranda planted her hands on the chest-high, brick windowsill and hoisted her body. Luckily, the glass had been completely knocked out of the window, but Miranda could feel small shards of it piercing her palms.

She tried to tell herself it was a game. She was a kid again, playing hide-and-seek with her neighborhood buddies. No one could ever beat her at that game.

With athletic ease, Miranda pulled her upper body through the hole, planting her bloody hands on the kitchen counter below her. She held her breath and cautiously slithered her lower body through, maneuvering herself sideways onto the counter. She froze as Henry's voice boomed from the next room. He was yelling toward the street again, ordering the police to get lost before he started shooting.

Keep talking, Henry, old boy.

Miranda let her feet down to the floor as quietly as she could, taking advantage of the noise coming from the next room. Retrieving her gun again, she tiptoed toward the kitchen doorway. She knew the hallway was about eight feet in length before it opened to the living room. Thankfully, the floors were carpeted.

Miranda's gut told her it would all come down to a duel. One of them would be dead before this was all over. But the thought that it might be her just wasn't one of the possibilities. All that mattered was getting Miki out alive.

Creeping along, Miranda silently prayed with each step that the floorboards beneath the carpet wouldn't squeak. At least if Henry suddenly made a move toward the hallway, she would hear him, since he weighed well over two hundred pounds.

Breathing steadily and as softly as she could, Miranda neared the archway to the living room. Just a few more inches and she'd be able to see beyond the wall. Slowly she crept, the minutes feeling like hours.

"C'mon Henry, they're not going to leave," she heard Miki plead.

She's okay! Miranda's heart pounded in relief. *All right, be cool now. You can do this.*

" —so why don't you just give it up?"

A sick hollowness pulled at Miranda's gut, a reminder that she'd probably left her stomach back on the kitchen counter. Inching her face closer to the edge, she could now see with one eye that Henry Wright was still at the window, his shotgun in his right hand. The rest of the room was blocked from view. She couldn't see where Miki was.

"Just shut up, pig. Do you want to die, huh?" he screamed. He had turned and was looking down at the floor somewhere to Miranda's left. The aim would be clear.

It was now or never. Sucking in a deep breath, Miranda sprang out, planting herself in a combat stance and aiming straight at Henry Wright.

"Police! Drop it, Henry, now!" Her jaw was set in steely resolve, her eyes focused and deadly. *C'mon, drop it you motherfucker!*

The man's eyes widened in shock, and his fleshy jowls dropped.

"I said drop it or I'll shoot!"

But he didn't drop it. And as though his actions were slowed to freeze-frame, he swung the gun toward Miranda, his mouth curled into a smirk, his eyes wild.

But he wasn't fast enough. Miranda pulled the trigger, and pulled it again and again, the explosions ripping through the room, momentarily deafening her. Somebody screamed. Her cylinder empty, she finally stopped, still frozen in position, the smell of gunpowder burning her nostrils. Her victim lay writhing on the floor, his gun innocuously beside him.

"Don't move, Henry," Miranda commanded, inching closer with her gun still trained on him. It was then she noticed her hand quivering.

With her free hand, Miranda retrieved the portable radio from her belt and snapped it on, remembering they might all be mincemeat if her coworkers outside thought Henry had just shot his hostages.

"Portable McCauley to all units," she breathed into it, nearly whispering. She barely felt the energy now to even talk as her adrenaline quickly receded.

"I'm in the house. Situation is under control and Ten-ninety-two has been disarmed. I need an ambulance."

"Miranda," Miki gasped, threatening to mimic the sobbing Shirley Wright, who hadn't moved from her position in the corner. "How . . ." She mumbled incoherently. Without taking her eyes or her gun off Henry, Miranda sidled over to Miki and unlocked her handcuffs.

"Jesus, McCauley, how the hell did you get in here?" asked an incredulous Jeff Rowe as he burst through the front door.

She sank to her knees and let her gun slip to the floor, the realization that she'd shot a man and had almost been shot herself dizzying her. Her head dipped, and she felt her mind go numb as nausea rose through her. She thought for sure she'd puke. She didn't even notice the others stampeding into the room.

Everything melted away into a whirling pool of nothingness, but the soothing arms of Miki suddenly squeezed her shoulders.

"Miranda," Miki sobbed. "I thought I was . . . that you . . ."

Miranda closed her eyes and fought back tears as she pulled Miki tightly into her in a protective embrace. Feeling Miki's trembling shoulders beneath her arms brought her out of her stupor. At least one of them had to be strong.

"I think you two better go to the hospital and get checked out," one of the ambulance attendants advised.

"And I'm gonna need your gun," piped up Detective Jim Clancy, who had arrived unnoticed with the rest of the growing traffic through the house. Miranda was vaguely aware of the noise level increasing.

She nodded as Clancy carefully picked up her gun from the floor and put it in a paper bag. The thought of all the red tape was too much for her to comprehend at the moment. She felt tiny against the forces now out of her control.

"C'mon, Miki." Miranda found her voice again. "Let's get out of here."

CHAPTER FOURTEEN

A visit to the hospital hadn't done either of them much good.

Miranda got her hands bandaged and a dose of free advice from a staff psychiatrist to come in and talk to her about the shooting as soon as possible.

Miki's thorough examination hadn't found anything to worry about, and she too was strongly advised to use the psychiatrist's services — all at the department's expense, of course. But Miki hadn't heard a word of it. She withdrew into herself and became a silent figure who simply nodded or shook her head when spoken to. She even seemed to shrink in size. To Miranda she looked pitiful, like a bedraggled, lost little animal.

Miranda took Miki back to her own house, figuring it'd be better for her in familiar surroundings. Both of them were in a state of shock. Miki was just plain numb, and Miranda was in a state of denial. Both could have used a strong shoulder, but for now they'd have to lean on each other.

"Are you hungry?" Miranda asked, once inside.

Miki shook her head, looking much older than her thirty years. Her face was puffy and pale, her eyes red and glassy.

"Is there anyone you'd like me to call for you?"

Again Miki shook her head. "Will you just stay here with me?"

Miranda pulled Miki into her, enveloping Miki's limp body in her strong arms.

"Of course. I'll stay as long as you like."

Miranda felt Miki's smooth hair brush against her chin and remembered how close she'd been to losing her just a few short hours ago. She tried to steady the tremble in her arms.

"Why don't you let me run you a bath and put you to bed."

Miranda felt as though she were talking to a child. When Miki didn't respond, she sat her down on the kitchen chair and turned the bathtub taps on.

Looking after Miki in her helpless state was just the therapy Miranda needed. She was glad Miki wanted her to stay. She could stay here and hide from Ken, Detective Clancy, pesky reporters and everyone else who would want to talk to her. She didn't want to deal with anyone, and Miki wasn't up for it either. So when the phone began ringing, they ignored it in an unspoken agreement.

Miranda expertly removed Miki's· uniform and guided her to the tub and its foamy contents.

"You look good," Miranda whispered, meaning every word of it as she drank in the smooth curves, the goose bumps on naked flesh, the inviting, familiar softness.

Miki's body was as exciting as she remembered. Miranda resisted the urge to stroke it, knowing the electricity would still be there, ready to shoot a flame of excitement through her body. The years they'd spent apart were quickly evaporating.

A faint recognition of — what, past memories, sexual attraction? — swept Miki's face, but it was gone again in a flash. She closed her eyes and lay motionless as Miranda reached into the warm water and gently scrubbed her, careful not to let the water touch her bandaged palms.

The early morning sun was streaming through Miki's bedroom window, but the blind soon put an abrupt end to that.

Miranda led Miki to the bed, suddenly aware of her own exhaustion.

"Will you lie with me?" Miki pleaded, her eyes blank.

Miki's fingernails dug into Miranda's shoulder as they lay together on the bed. She clutched tightly as though Miranda were her lifeline, which was fitting, Miranda supposed.

"You won't leave me, will you?" Miki whispered, barely audible, into Miranda's neck.

Miranda tightened her grip on Miki. "I'll be here for as long as you want me to be."

Miranda closed her eyes. Images of Henry Wright turning his shotgun on her played in her mind like a horror movie she was being forced to watch. He was smirking, almost laughing. Then the roar of her own gun firing. She'd even lost count of the number of times she fired. She shot until the gun clicked empty. Then the groaning, the faint smell of blood. Someone screaming.

Miranda forced her eyes open. She didn't even know if Henry Wright was dead or alive. She thought he'd been alive when they took him out, but she couldn't be sure now.

She stroked Miki's hair. Her fingertips slid down to the soft hairs on the nape of her neck, drawing tiny circles, barely touching. The faint smell of soap reached Miranda's nostrils, and she inhaled deeply, letting her exhaled breath ruffle Miki's soft hair.

If only things were so simple, so real as this, Miranda thought, her chest welling with love for Miki. She knew now it was the kind of love that knew no confines of time or space, as though Miranda had loved her all her life. Yes, I have loved her all my life!

"I love you, Miki," she whispered to the sleeping woman in her arms. A tear spilled down Miranda's cheek and onto Miki. She'd never had the courage to say those words to her. To anyone for that matter, not even to the man she was supposed to marry.

Oh, Christ, Ken.

Miranda felt nauseous. How could she even think of spending another day with Ken now, after what she and Miki had been through. He could never understand in a million years what it's like coming so close to losing someone you love — the taste of fear in your mouth, the throbbing of your heart in your throat, wondering if your heart could even keep beating if you got to her too late. No, of course he wouldn't understand, and the sight of him would remind her of that every time.

Miranda felt her career aspirations dwindling fast. It just didn't matter anymore. Not the promotion, Ken, none of it. It had all ceased mattering the instant she knew Miki was in trouble. Nothing was too big a risk when it came to Miki. Whatever the price, it didn't matter. She'd pay it with interest.

Miranda felt the golf ball–sized lump in her throat thickening, and the tears came quickly. *How could I have been so stupid all this time? How could I have given Miki up for a career that could all be over now anyway?* Her career, or at least her chance for promotion, might be gone forever if her superiors felt she'd used excessive force. They could teach you every textbook method until you had them cold. But no gunman, no rapist, no crazy person ever followed the script exactly. You drew on things you were taught and your own experiences, and hoped like hell it worked. And if the public or your superiors didn't like the consequences, you could be tossed behind bars right along with the very people you tried to keep off the streets. Her grandfather and other old-time cops had always told her the line was a thin one between a cop and a criminal. She never believed it until now.

Miranda's tears ebbed. Exhaustion tugged at her, and she closed her eyes.

* * * * *

It was nightfall when Miki stirred again. They'd both slept soundly, nestled together like perfectly matched spoons.

Miranda was sleepily aware of eyes staring at her and finally opened hers.

They stared, silent and unblinking, their bodies touching. Neither moved. Each studied the other, trading mute explorations of each other's souls.

Miranda felt translucent and defenseless, even more so than the time Miki had consoled her after she'd been dumped by Taylor Whiteside. With each passing moment she felt the thin wall around her soul melt under Miki's warm gaze, and she yielded to it. It felt safe. More than that, it felt necessary.

Miki's index finger began tracing an invisible line down Miranda's hairline at her temple. Down it slid to her ear, then tenderly followed her jawline.

Gone from Miki's eyes was the faraway, clouded look. She gazed intensely, desperately probing Miranda's soul, searching for a sign of reciprocation.

A trace of a smile formed on Miranda's lips, and she gently brought Miki's finger to her mouth. She kissed Miki's fingertip before her tongue reached out and snatched it, drawing it into her mouth. Miranda sucked on Miki's finger seductively, tugging at it with her tongue, alternately licking and sucking on it.

Miki's heart skipped a beat and her thoughts began to gel for the first time in hours. *Miranda wants me!*

She felt the familiar swelling between her legs as wetness trickled onto her inner thigh. Miki squeezed her legs together, trying to smother the persistent throbbing.

She sucked in her breath, and this time the ache in her heart matched the one between her legs. *I can't go through this again.* She closed her eyes, a wave of panic rising through her.

"What's the matter?" Miranda whispered between gentle kisses. It felt so good to kiss Miki again.

Miki balked, searching for the right words. "I don't think I can go through this again."

Miranda's brow knitted in confusion. "Go through what?"

Miki felt a teardrop filling the corner of her eye. "You loving me, then . . ." She couldn't finish. It hurt too much.

Miranda ignored the unfinished thought and stifled Miki's misgivings with a ferocious kiss. Her mouth pushed hard, forcing Miki's lips apart just enough to slip her tongue in. Miranda pushed with her body, too, until she was on top of Miki, her mouth forcing Miki's head deeper into the pillow, her tongue dancing demandingly inside, penetrating deeply.

Miranda moaned as her body and tongue pumped in furious synchronization, grinding into Miki. She was fucking Miki's mouth with her tongue. God, she wanted Miki like she'd never wanted her before. She didn't even care if Miki wanted her back. She would have her, right here, right now. There was no room for gentleness or loving pillow talk, not after more than three years of slowly dying inside, and after almost losing each other to a crazed gunman. Miranda was desperate to reaffirm her need to make love with a woman again, the need to feel whole again. And she fiercely needed to capture Miki's body, more as proof to herself that she would never again let it go or take Miki for granted.

Miranda selfishly ignored the mild, muffled protestations from Miki. Roughly, she jerked Miki's robe apart with her right hand. Her left arm moved across Miki's chest, forming a viselike clamp in case she tried to rise up. Her free hand moved down; expertly she parted Miki's lips before mercilessly jamming two fingers deep into her.

Miki's body jerked back in surprise, but Miranda only pushed harder, slick fingers darting in and out. A sheen of sweat began to form across Miranda's forehead as her entire body pumped against Miki. She was panting for breath now.

Miranda's wet mouth latched onto Miki's left breast. She licked the already erect nipple, then rigorously sucked, at times almost enveloping Miki's entire breast with her mouth.

A low, guttural moan escaped from Miki. Miranda's incessant hunger for her was undeniably turning her on. Miki's head screamed at her to stop Miranda before it was too late, before she fell for her all over again (as if she had ever stopped). But her throbbing vagina yearned for Miranda's driving, jabbing fingers. Even in Miki's wildest fantasies Miranda had never wanted her so desperately. She felt her own wetness coat Miranda's fingers and trickle onto the sheets.

A drop of Miranda's sweat fell onto Miki's breast. It hovered unsteadily as if contemplating which side to give into. Finally it spilled into a little trail down the side of Miki's breast and down past her ribs.

"Oh, Miranda," Miki gasped from that distant

state between reality and total, pleasured abandonment.

Her hips began pushing back at Miranda, demanding more. And Miranda gave it to her, driving to Miki's hilt over and over again until the whole bed began knocking into the wall in perfect time. She was breathing hard over Miki, her body and hand thrusting into Miki until it seemed she would explode inside Miki. Her thumb reached for Miki's clitoris.

Miki had never been so forcefully — and thoroughly — fucked before. She sucked in her breath, and it escaped in a near scream as her pelvis thrust up one last time, holding for a moment before her body jerked violently. Her whole body seemed to exhale in relief before she collapsed in a shuddering heap.

Miranda hurried to hold her, feeling the quiet quivering beneath her. She thought Miki might be crying softly, but she didn't dare look. She just clutched her tightly.

"I love you, baby," Miranda whispered. She found herself choking back tears. "I don't want to lose you ever again."

Miki pulled back, unsure of what she'd just heard.

"Miranda," she answered, wide-eyed, not quite believing. "Do you know what you're saying?"

Miranda couldn't help but smile somewhat smugly. Yes, she'd said it, and what a relief it was to dump the weight she'd been carrying around for so long. Even the times she'd denied it was there, the burden had never escaped her before.

"I love you! Okay? I've never stopped loving you, and I'm just sorry it took all this time and us almost getting killed for me to say it," Miranda beamed.

"And now that I've said it, I'm never going to stop saying it!"

A tear trickled down Miki's cheek. She didn't yet dare show the joy Miranda's words had brought. "But your career and your life here and —"

"To hell with all that." Miranda held Miki's face. "You tell me this. What the hell good are a few stripes on your arm if you're dead? And if I'd lost you last night, I might as well be dead." She hesitated, her voice cracking with emotion.

Miki recognized the determination in Miranda's tone. It was the same tenacity Miranda displayed when she talked about how much her career meant to her. Only now she was saying how little it meant.

"I just want us to be together, and it took this hostage thing for me to realize how important you are to me. And if I can't have you *and* my career," Miranda's lips pursed for a moment, "well then, I guess I'll be looking for a new job."

Miki felt delirious. She'd always hoped, even dreamed, that Miranda would one day say those very words to her, even though she grudgingly admitted to herself it would probably never happen. Her closest friends back home had told her as much when her pining for Miranda reached irritating proportions. She'd pretty much given up hope. Yet here was Miranda, lying in her bed, pledging her love to her.

Tenderly, she kissed Miranda, tasting her lips and gently tugging on them with her own, until their kissing became more frenetic. The need to seal, or consummate, their newfound bond took on an energy all its own as they lost themselves in each other's bodies again.

Miki fumbled with the buttons on Miranda's shirt.

All this time she had never taken her uniform off, which by now was badly wrinkled and limp with sweat.

"No, wait, I should take a shower," Miranda protested.

By now Miki had removed the shirt and cast it to the floor. She was working on the Velcro straps of Miranda's bulletproof vest.

"We can shower later. I don't want to waste another minute."

The sight of Miranda's compact but firm breasts nearly took Miki's breath away. The broad shoulders, the hard pectoral muscles. How could she have forgotten how truly wonderful Miranda's naked body was? The fine details had begun to fade from her memories and fantasies after such a long absence. But Miki's fingertips familiarly danced across Miranda's soft neck to the fleshy hollow where her collarbone began. She was firmly toned, yet bright red in anticipation, and Miki unconsciously licked her lips.

"Oh, Miranda, you're incredible!"

Miki gently covered Miranda's neck with lingering kisses, taking her time, as though her mission were to cover every inch of Miranda's body with her lips. She wanted to savor the taste and the texture of every part of Miranda, and as she did so, she silently vowed to remember the taste of her, the feel of her, forever.

Miranda moaned and squirmed impatiently, wanting more, and wanting it now. But she'd have to wait, Miki smiled to herself.

Miki's tongue drew faint, wet circles around Miranda's breast, slowly closing in on her nipple like a bulls-eye. When it finally tackled its game, it teased and tantalized, lingered, then hesitated before falling back to the same pattern over and over. Punctuating each pattern, Miki's mouth frantically sucked Miranda's breast.

"Oh, Jesus, Miki, I want you . . . c'mon!" Miranda screamed out, her moaning keeping pace with her heightened breathing.

Miki ignored the plea, moving down to Miranda's firm stomach. Her tongue teasingly played with Miranda's belly button then, what seemed like hours later, Miki carefully unzipped Miranda's trousers and began easing them down over her hips.

In a fit of impatience, Miranda reached down and roughly yanked her pants down past her knees, then kicked them off.

"In a hurry?" Miki winked.

Miranda's underpants were sticking to her. She felt she'd surely explode any minute now, and Miki hadn't even got under them yet. She tried to rein herself in, not wanting to cheat herself of Miki's touch, Miki's tongue . . . *oh, God, that tongue!*

Miranda dragged her hand across her forehead to wipe away the fresh sweat gathering there. With her wet fingers, she reached down and stroked Miki's head as it hovered over her stomach. Gently, Miranda nudged Miki's head toward her throbbing clitoris, then pushed more forcefully as Miki devilishly resisted. She couldn't take the torment any more, and just as she thought she'd collapse into a heap of raw frustration, Miki's tongue plunged inside her creamy, pliant passage.

Miranda threw her head back deep into the pillow and squeezed her eyes shut. Her lungs pumped in unity with Miki's thrusting tongue, and for a few seconds she lingered in a surreal state, enjoying the pleasure surging through her legs right up her spine. Miki's tongue skillfully massaged her clitoris, and the light show began behind Miranda's eyelids. First purple, then brilliant orange and yellow shapes darted across her visionary field. Her body felt as though it were being sucked through a tunnel, and it prickled with pleasure.

Miranda drew in a deep breath and held it as her hips uncontrollably pushed into Miki's mouth. Then came the slow rumble, gathering at her knees and pulsating powerfully as it rose through her body. She shook with each electrifying wave as a kaleidoscope of colors burst in her mind. Her fists had clenched into tight balls, and she exhaled in a loud burst.

They held each other and fell asleep in a naked embrace, emotional and physical exhaustion holding them in its grip. They awoke a few hours later as cracks of early morning sunshine peeked through the edges of the shade.

Miki's hand moved to caress Miranda's breast. But Miranda gently pushed it away and sat up.

"What's wrong?" Miki asked, concern heavy in her voice.

Miranda leaned over and kissed her.

"It's okay, honey. I need to go. There're some things I have to take care of."

"Stay with me. I want to make love to you again," Miki pleaded. "I don't want you to be away from me again, not even for just a little while."

"I know, and believe me, I want to spend every minute with you too. But I need to tie up some loose ends."

She slid out of bed and began pulling on her crumpled uniform. She wrinkled her nose at it in disgust.

"You mean Ken?" Miki sighed.

"Yeah, Ken. And work. They'll be wanting a statement from me. From you, too."

"But right now?" Miki's insecurity was palpable.

Miranda sat down on the bed and took Miki's hand in hers. She traced an abstract design on her palm with her fingertips.

"I want a clean slate for us. Then I promise, I'll be back, and I'll be back to stay. I love you, honey. Will you be okay for a few hours?"

Miki nodded and fought back tears. She felt so dependent, like a child, but she knew Miranda was right. "I'll miss you."

"I'll miss you, too."

Miranda kissed her again, then quickly left before she changed her mind.

CHAPTER FIFTEEN

A sick feeling gnawed at Miranda's insides as she pulled her truck into Ken's driveway. Emotional confrontations made her feel that way, and she usually tried her best to avoid them or put them off as long as possible, the way she'd done with Ken these past weeks. But getting him out of the picture now was urgent. So she plowed ahead with the single-minded persistence that was her trademark.

"Miranda!" Ken greeted her in surprise. "Oh, darling, I heard about the shooting! Are you okay?"

Miranda stepped in, and Ken shut the door behind her. *Of course I'm not okay,* she thought contemptuously. *What a stupid question!* She sighed inwardly, then softened. It wasn't his fault. How could he know what to say?

Miranda absently ran her hand through her short hair, her face unreadable. "I'm doing okay, for now."

Ken took her by the elbow and led her to the couch. They sat. He clutched her bandaged hands and wrinkled his forehead with worry.

Then the words tumbled out. "I've been trying to reach you ever since I heard. And Chief Burridge has been looking for you, too. Everyone's worried. Where've you been?"

Miranda had to squelch the impish smile she felt as she thought about the last several hours she'd spent with Miki. Then she began remembering what had brought them to Miki's place. She frowned worriedly and chewed her lip.

Miranda stared at her hand interlocked with his. "I stayed with Miki Paxton. She needed someone — she needed me — after what happened."

Secretly, Ken was hurt that Miranda hadn't turned to him after such a trauma. She had totally avoided him. Just days ago she'd said she needed time to herself to think about things, but surely that didn't apply when something like this happened. It worried him, and at the same time, he knew deep down that it was just another sign things were over between them. If she couldn't turn to him for comfort after what was probably the single most traumatic thing in her life, well then, just what was there between them?

"What about you?" he asked, thrusting thoughts of her well-being ahead of his insecurities.

Miranda shrugged. She'd been doing a fairly good job of ignoring the shooting. First Miki had needed her, then they'd rediscovered each other. And now Ken. She'd compartmentalized her emotions, and right now there was just no room for dealing with the shooting. When she *was* ready to deal with it, it certainly wouldn't be with him.

"I'm hanging in," she finally answered evenly. "Right now I have to focus on assisting with the investigation. I don't think it'd help anybody if I just fell apart."

Ken nodded. "I was worried sick about you. I'm glad you're doing okay, but I'm still concerned."

He hugged her, and her body stiffened in response.

"Ken, we need to talk about us," Miranda blurted out, pulling away.

Ken shrank back in shock. She wanted to talk about *them*? That's why she was here, to talk about their relationship after she'd been nearly shot to death? Not to say that she was okay, or to soothe his worries. No, she wanted to talk about their bloody engagement! He felt panicked. His mouth dry, he gulped, then acquiesced with a nod.

Miranda sat back and corralled her strength. This was it. This was where she crossed that dreaded line. No more being two different people — one behind closed doors, the other a contrived image. There was a need in her now to be true to herself, and that meant loving Miki with everything she had.

"I can't marry you, Ken, not now and not ever. In fact, I'll never get married."

Ken was horrified. He hadn't expected her to be so blunt. And what was that last bit? What the hell was she talking about?

"Wh-why not?" he stammered. "What do you mean you'll never get married?"

Everyone got married sooner or later, Ken believed. That was what people did. It was certainly expected of him, and he knew he would fulfill that expectation. From a very young age, his father had made clear what was expected of him. He would get a good education, work hard, establish himself in the family business, then think about marrying and having children. Who was he to question the order?

"Ken, some people just aren't meant for that lifestyle, and I'm one of them."

"I don't understand," he said, his head shaking in confusion. "If you love someone, you get married. Are you saying you don't love me?"

Miranda was losing control of the conversation. She shifted uncomfortably. "I do love you, Ken. I think you're a great guy. But I don't have the kind of love for you that a woman needs to have for the man she's going to marry."

Again, he veered the focus to her love, or lack of love, for him. He couldn't help but take it all personally. "But maybe with a little more time you could. I mean, we've only been together a little more than a year —"

"No, Ken," Miranda interrupted forcefully. "I can't ever love you or any man that way." She drew in her breath as if she'd need every ounce of it to push out her words. "I'm a lesbian, Ken."

Ken felt his mouth drop open, then he firmly clamped it shut, not even sure he'd heard her right. For once in his life his mind was a total blank. Everything seemed to stand still.

"It wouldn't be fair to you or me if we just continued with something that isn't right," Miranda continued. "Don't you see?"

No, he didn't see. He didn't see at all. Miranda couldn't be a lesbian — she'd slept with him, after all, and even seemed to enjoy it. Sure she was a little masculine, but she wasn't like those women he'd occasionally run into at the lumber store who were three feet wide and walked around in work boots, flannel jackets, and ball caps. Now those were lesbians. Miranda? Nah!

Ken's mind raced, trying to grasp what he couldn't possibly understand. What made Miranda think she was a lesbian, for God's sake? Did she feel the need to experiment, was that it? Had he not been man enough —?

His mind burned with questions, yet he couldn't get them out of his mouth. "Are you sure about this?" was all he could manage.

Miranda nodded firmly. "I'm sorry I wasn't honest with you, Ken. But I wasn't even being honest with myself."

"So, you're attracted to women or what?" His tone was slightly contemptuous, impatient, needing to understand something he was incapable of. Again his mind searched for past clues. He never noticed Miranda gawking or leering at other women or commenting on women's bodies or anything like that. Come to think of it, though, she never gawked at good-looking men either.

Now it was Miranda's turn to be impatient. She didn't exactly feel she was an expert on the matter. The only other lesbians she'd ever really known were Taylor Whiteside and Miki.

"It's more than just a physical attraction, Ken. It's ... I don't know, everything." She spread her hands out in frustration. "I just feel more *connected* to women."

Ken absently rubbed his forehead. Why was she doing this to him? Why had she even agreed to marry him in the first place? At least some of it was making sense now — her pulling away from him these last few weeks, their lack of sexual intimacy.

"Is there someone else, Miranda?"

"No," Miranda lied. No need to bring Miki into this right now. She had enough on her plate. Besides, bringing a third person into the picture would just confuse the issue more. She didn't want Ken to simplify things and think she'd just substituted someone else for him. Miranda didn't believe in breaking up with one person simply to be with another. That was a cop-out, a distraction from the real issue. You broke up with someone because the relationship wasn't working. Period. The third person was just a manifestation of an unhealthy relationship.

Miranda stood up, knowing there wasn't much else to say. She hoped they could still be friends, or at least not enemies. But he'd need time to digest all of this. After all, it'd taken her years to reach this conclusion, yet he'd only had minutes to comprehend it.

"I'm sorry, Ken. I didn't mean to hurt you. Please believe that."

Ken stood too, but he was silent. He looked crestfallen, and it was too early to say just how accepting or understanding he might be.

They stood there in silence, both feeling more awkward with each second. Finally Miranda turned and walked to the door.

Leaving, she felt strangely relieved yet anxious. Though she felt freer, she knew in her gut it would be no less frightening now. There was a nagging feeling that things were just starting.

Ken slumped back on the couch, his trembling hands covering his face. Her words had been a kick in the stomach. She couldn't do this to him, embarrass him like that. She just *couldn't*!

His eyes stared from between fanned fingers. *You'll pay for this, for making a fool of me. Oh, yes, one way or the other, you'll pay.*

It took about two hours with Detective Clancy and Deputy Chief Fairborn to go over the hostage-taking events. Technically, Miranda would stay off duty until the investigation was over, which she was assured would be soon.

Miranda also learned that Henry Wright hadn't died, at least not yet. But he was in pretty bad shape, they'd said. He'd been hit four times. Miranda had remained curiously detached, going through the

192

motions and uttering terse replies as though someone else inhabited her body.

"Miranda," the chief beckoned on her way out.

Miranda was led into his office, and found Jane Fulsome occupying a chair. She rose, strode earnestly to Miranda, and shook her hand.

"We've been very worried about you. How are you holding up?" she asked with concern.

"I'm holding up fine, thank you."

Burridge smiled and motioned for Miranda to sit down. "Well, I want you to take as much time as you need, and that goes for Constable Paxton too." A slow grin made its way across his face as they all took seats. "Miranda, I want you to know you did us all proud. You showed tremendous courage, and you saved lives in there."

"I may have taken one, too," she mumbled, looking away.

"Nonsense," Burridge said, waving his hand. "You did what you had to do to save the life of an officer. That's what I like, Miranda, an officer who knows how to improvise when the chips are down. Constable Paxton could have been long dead before the tactical team got there. And the other hostage as well."

Jane nodded, smiling. "Our Member of Parliament contacted me this morning, Constable McCauley. Today in the House, she's going to nominate you for the Governor General's Medal of Bravery."

She waited for a reaction from Miranda, but got none.

"You were very brave, and you make all of Hooperstown proud."

"Thank you," Miranda shrugged without feeling. Inside, she was incredulous that they could talk about medals at a time like this. She had just done her job, for God's sake. And if it had been anyone else but Miki in there, she probably wouldn't have done it. It wasn't bravery so much as love.

The chief and the board chair looked at each other, unsure of what to say next.

"I really should be on my way. I want to check in on Miki."

Miranda stood and they watched her go, knowing she was still shell-shocked, but not really understanding.

Burridge smiled at Jane. "She's a lock."

"The promotion?"

Burridge nodded. In a few days, he, Fulsome, and Fairborn would be making their official recommendation to the police board, which would rubber-stamp the decision. The board rarely fought the subcommittee's recommendation, and even if it did, the motion only needed a majority to pass. With Burridge, Fairborn, and Fulsome on her side, it was just a formality.

"Do you concur?" Burridge added.

Jane smiled. "Of course. Have you seen the papers? This city loves her. I think we'd be imprudent to overlook her."

CHAPTER SIXTEEN

The smell of cigars and the sounds of clinking ice cubes and pool cues knicking billiard balls greeted Jackson Burridge as he entered the lounge of the Hooperstown Golf and Country Club. The lounge was for men only, and that was just fine with the police chief. It meant you could have a few drinks, a few smokes, and talk business or politics without interruption.

"Hello, Jackson." The mayor, Ken Cardwell Sr.,

stood with outstretched hand, a smoldering fat Cuban cigar nesting in the other.

Shaking his hand, Burridge beamed and sat down.

"I've already taken the liberty of ordering a Scotch for you," Cardwell smiled and nodded toward the glass in front of Burridge. Scotch was his own favorite, not the chief's. But that was irrelevant.

"Thank you for meeting me here, Jackson. We haven't had a drink together in a while." Cardwell raised his glass. "Cheers!"

"Cheers," Burridge echoed, raising his own glass and sipping tentatively.

"So," Cardwell continued between puffs. "We'll be meeting later this week on the sergeant's promotion, no?" Cardwell, as mayor, was a voting member of the police board.

"That's right."

Cardwell paused, squinting, looking reflectively into his glass. He was immaculate in his tailored three-piece suit and his perfectly barbered, thick gray hair. Even his cologne smelled of money.

"And has the subcommittee made a decision?"

Burridge grinned, knowing Cardwell would be pleased his future daughter-in-law had it in the bag. "Yes, as a matter of fact. Hooperstown's own hero, and your soon-to-be daughter-in-law."

But the chief's grin faded at the sight of the mayor's hardening face. Cardwell scratched his chin unhappily.

"Are you sure about your choice, Jackson?"

Burridge shrugged innocently. "Of course. We feel she's the best one for the job, and with what happened —"

Cardwell shook his head impatiently. "What I

mean is, have you really looked into her character? Because I think if you do, well . . ." The mayor held back, hoping he wouldn't need to spell it out.

"I'm sorry, Ken, I don't know what you're getting at."

Cardwell stared unhappily at the chief as if he had to explain the very obvious to a child. "You see, Jackson, she's no longer engaged to my son, thank God." The last part came out as a mumble.

"Why?" Burridge looked worried. "What's happened?"

Cardwell smiled now, the smile of a shark zeroing in on its prey. "She's not the marrying type, if you know what I mean."

Seeing the confused look on the chief's face, he leaned closer and leered, beginning to enjoy himself. "She likes *pussy,* Jackson." He drew deeply on his cigar, his eyes beady and glinting.

Burridge's mouth was in his lap. Surely the mayor couldn't be serious, for God's sake!

Cardwell sat back, his mouth curling down into an ugly snarl. "Certainly you can understand why we wouldn't want that —" he waved his cigar in the air "— *sort* in a position of authority."

Burridge was still stunned and simply nodded.

Cardwell smiled again, instantly the picture of politeness. "So, I understand you'll be putting a budget request in to council soon for a couple of new marked cars and a new computer system." He sipped his drink and winked. "Somehow I don't think that'll be a problem."

* * * * *

197

Miranda spotted Jeff Rowe right away in the small cafe. He was the only customer sitting alone.

"Miranda," he stood. She shook his hand suspiciously.

She'd been surprised when he called to ask her to lunch. They weren't exactly buddies, and he hadn't spoken to her since the shooting. But what the hell, something had to be up.

A waitress flew past and dropped a couple of menus on their table. Rowe studied his as though it were a chemistry textbook while Miranda barely glanced at hers.

"That was quite the job you did last week, rescuing Miki Paxton the way you did," he finally mumbled, still staring into his menu.

Miranda didn't answer.

"Tell me, Miranda," he continued, this time putting his menu down and looking at her. "Would you have done that for just anyone?"

Miranda sat back and crossed her arms over her chest, waiting for him to blink first. He did.

"I mean, what's her secret? What's she got?"

Miranda smiled, but her eyes were driving a fist into his face. Of course he knows. He's a friend of Ken's, for Christ's sake! But he could play his games on someone else's time. "What do you want, Jeff?"

He smiled back, full of himself and his false sense of power. "The board makes its decision tomorrow night on the promotion."

"Yes, I'd heard that."

"I think you should pull out, Miranda. It'd be the

— what should I say — *manly* thing to do, don't you think?"

Miranda glowered. She'd had it up to here with the prick. She didn't give a shit about the promotion, but she'd be damned if she'd pull out for the benefit of some homophobic, misogynist asshole like him.

"What the hell are you talking about?"

The waitress swung by again but made a hasty retreat after hearing Miranda's tone.

He savored the sweet taste of victory in his mouth.

"What I'm saying is, someone of your persuasion just wouldn't cut it, at least not in this town."

"Go on," Miranda prodded, daring him to spit it out.

He squirmed a bit now and had a hard time meeting her eye. "Look, I'm just trying to do you a favor. I don't think the guys would be too happy about having a dyke in charge. Nor would the brass."

Miranda stood and leaned across the table, her face inches from his, her eyes giving him that you're-a-speck-of-shit-in-a-cesspool look.

"No, but I'll bet they'd be real happy to have some heartless, ball-less asshole like you in charge. And I've got more of both than you, Rowe."

Jeff Rowe smirked, then finally laughed contemptuously in her face. "I'll bet Miki thinks so, too."

Miranda felt her temper snap like a twig at the mention of her lover's name. She grabbed him by the collar and the knot of his tie, squeezing, all the time knowing she was playing right into his hands, but not caring. "You can go straight to hell, Rowe."

She stormed out, rage swirling around her. Like specks of paper in a windstorm, people fluttered and floated in her wake.

"Everybody knows," she heard him yell as she nearly shoved the door off its hinges.

Miranda walked past her truck and kept going. She zipped her leather coat up against the damp November air. She hated this time of year the most. Once the snow fell and the dry cold set in, winter was beautiful, peaceful. But November was so gray and barren, and lonely somehow. She felt a strange kinship with the dull sky and fallow trees, their branches stiff against the cold.

There had never been a time when she didn't care about her career, her future, about what people thought. Miki loved her, and she loved Miki more than anything in the world. And she would be with Miki at all costs — she hadn't wavered on that since the shooting. But it was all so damned scary, so foreign, so out of her control.

Miranda walked past a schoolyard, studying the chain-link fence as it blurred past, counting the aluminum posts. She knew she was walking toward Miki's house, to the woman she loved and to the comfort her soul craved. She just hoped Miki could soothe the dull ache she felt in the pit of her very being.

Miranda plunked down on a wood bench in the small park across from Miki's. She had to sort through her feelings before she went to Miki. She needed to find some answers and, like always, she'd find them alone.

Maybe Jeff Rowe was right. Maybe she should go to the chief and withdraw her name from consideration. It'd save them all a big hassle. At least she'd still have a job, and if she kept a lid on things, her coworkers would probably leave her and Miki alone. It was a hell of a lot worse for gay male cops, Miranda knew.

"Want some company?"

It was Miki, hands jammed into her denim jacket pockets, blond head tilted to the side, a half-smile on her pretty face.

Though she didn't feel like smiling, Miranda couldn't help it. Miki did that to her. She slid over to make room.

Miki sat, and without a word, put her arm behind Miranda and pulled her into her shoulder. "Want to talk about it?"

Miranda shrugged, not looking at her.

"How did lunch go?"

"Oh, just wonderful," Miranda answered facetiously. She sat up straight and looked at Miki. "Rowe thinks I should make a quiet retreat with my tail between my legs."

Miki's eyes widened for just a moment. "So it's come to this, already."

Miranda shrugged again. "Maybe he's right."

Miki didn't like what she was hearing. The shooting had made Miranda realize that her life, and Miki's, and their life together, was more important than her career. But it wasn't like her to just walk away from a fight, to walk away from something she knew was unfair. As a cop, Miki knew Miranda would never walk away from someone who had been unfairly victimized. So why should she abandon herself?

"Is that what you really think, Miranda? Do you think you're not capable of being a sergeant because you're gay?"

"Of course not."

Miki knew in her heart Miranda still clutched at the hope that she could have her career and her promotions. But she'd lost the drive to fight for it.

"Do you think you wouldn't be able to cope with all the gossiping, all the finger pointing? Is that it?"

Miranda shrugged. "I don't know. I've never had to before."

Miki took Miranda's hand and squeezed it. The bandages were gone now, but her palm was still tender and scarred. "You still want the promotion, don't you?"

Miranda felt her eyes moisten. Miki had always forced her to be honest with herself, even when it wasn't pleasant.

"Yeah, I guess I do. But not at any cost." She looked into Miki's gray-blue eyes and squeezed back. "I'm not giving you up again."

Miki's face opened in a big smile. "Then let's fight the bastards."

Miranda, in full-dress uniform, stood as the double oak doors opened, her hat in her hands. Miki, in black wool slacks and silk shirt, stood too, as the five police board members strode through the waiting area. They hadn't noticed the two women at first.

"Hello Constable McCauley, Constable Paxton," Jane Fulsome smiled, walking up to them. She shook their hands warmly.

Ken Cardwell Sr. plainly ignored Miranda and continued on into the meeting room. Miranda nodded to the chief, who, after a moment's hesitation, gave a slight nod back. No one was smiling, except for Jane. But hers quickly vanished at the thickening tension in the room.

She searched Miranda's face for clues, the others having hastily moved off to the adjoining conference room. But Miranda seemed as perplexed as she. Without another word, Jane hurried off to the meeting, steeling herself for what was fast beginning to feel like an unpleasant chore.

"Gentlemen, shall we begin?" she nodded to the sour faces before her. She decided to ignore the frowns and furtive glances; she'd come to know what it was all about sooner or later.

Miranda paced in the waiting area, stopping occasionally near the double doors. But they were too thick to let any sound through.

Miki, seated on the leather couch, tapped her foot nervously to some inaudible beat.

Both felt helpless, but they would have felt even more helpless had they stayed home. They had to be here, to assess the faces as they emerged from the meeting, to see the spurious eyes of those who'd just slammed to a halt such a promising career. And Miranda knew they'd do it, especially after seeing the trapped look on the chief's face and the arrogant aloofness in the man who would have been her father-in-law.

But they were ready for it. They'd already arranged for a local newspaper reporter to show up at meeting's end, and they'd made contact with a big-city lawyer who promised to serve a lawsuit on the city of Hooperstown and the Hooperstown police force for discrimination if they turned her down. Sure, it might be hard to prove their decision was based on homophobic principles, but they'd sure as hell make these bastards squirm.

"You know, I think Jane Fulsome's on our side," Miranda said, stopping in front of Miki. It was the most hopeful she'd sounded all day.

"Do you think she'd be willing to publicly admit why you were turned down, if it comes to that?"

Miranda chewed on a fingernail. "Whatever was going on with that bunch when they first came in here, she wasn't a part of it."

But neither knew if she'd have the moral courage to stand up for Miranda. They didn't know much about Jane. She'd only come back to Hooperstown to look after her sick, elderly parents shortly after Miranda had moved to town. But they did know she was a damned good lawyer, and her father had been a damned good appeals court judge — tough but fair, word had it. The Fulsomes were Hooperstown's favorite sons, and they had been for generations.

"Next on the agenda, gentlemen, is the sergeant's

promotion." Jane shuffled her papers, feeling a shadow settle over the room.

"Chief Burridge?" she nodded across the table. As chair of the three-member hiring committee, it was up to him to announce the recommendation to the board, even though Jane knew fully what it was.

Jackson Burridge cleared his throat nervously. He looked everywhere but at Jane. "Yes, well, the committee recommends for the position of sergeant, Constable Jeff Rowe."

Jane thought he'd simply made a slip of the tongue. She waited for the chief to correct his mistake, but only the thumping of the table by Mayor Cardwell broke the silence.

"I'll second that."

Jane's gray eyes peered from over her half-moon reading glasses and scanned the table: the mayor smiled smugly, Deputy Chief Fairborn squirmed and pretended to look through his papers, the chief stared into his folded hands. The other board member, Peter Bishop, looked totally bored and tapped his pen impatiently.

Jane ripped her glasses off and tossed them roughly to the table. The chief jumped. What the hell were these old boys up to? The three of them had already agreed to promote Miranda McCauley, and now Burridge and Fairborn were overriding her. She didn't like this little sideshow one bit.

Jane's voice smoldered. "Before we take this to a vote, Chief Burridge and Deputy Chief Fairborn, I'd like a moment with you."

She strode to the door that led to Burridge's adjoining office without waiting for them.

They shut the door as they came in, knowing, like naughty schoolboys, the verbal drubbing they were in for. Jane had that authoritative, indignant air about her. When she spoke, people sat up and listened.

She leaned against the desk, arms folded tautly across her chest. Her jaw tightened and she glared at Burridge, for she knew Fairborn was simply the sheep. "Correct me if I'm wrong, but did the three of us not decide we would recommend Constable McCauley for the promotion?"

Burridge glanced at the ceiling, hoping to find some courage there. "Yes. However, the deputy chief and I have had reasons to reassess our original recommendation."

Jane waited, unblinking. "I see. And you didn't think to include me in this new decision?"

"We didn't see the need to interrupt your busy schedule." Burridge's hands spread out in pleading fashion. "We didn't want to concern you."

Jane lidded her ballooning temper and curtly shook her head in disbelief. "You didn't want to concern me. Well, I'll tell you what concerns me, chief. What concerns me is your going behind my back in collusion with the mayor and others on this committee and making decisions in my absence."

Jane stood up straight, hands defiantly on her hips. She was a tall woman and stood nearly eye level with the chief, but her demeanor added inches to her height. She kept her voice low, the lethal sting in it enough. "I am chairing this board and I will not have decisions made behind my back. Is that understood?"

The chief swallowed, his head bobbing in a small nod.

"Now," she continued, hands relaxing behind her back. "What seems to be the sudden problem with McCauley?"

Burridge shifted for a moment, then straightened his shoulders, knowing he shouldn't be feeling guilty for what needed to be said. "Constable McCauley's a..." he paused, deliberating on what word to use, "...a homosexual."

Jane stood patiently, waiting for the other shoe to drop. Finally she shrugged, palms turned up questioningly. "You mean that's it?"

Burridge nodded, trying to work himself up in the face of this condescending, ball-breaking bitch. If it'd been up to him, he probably would have promoted Miranda anyway, providing word hadn't gotten out about her perversion. But if the mayor knew all about it, who else knew? He didn't want his department the laughingstock of the city.

"I think that's more than enough," he answered quietly.

Jane's eyes caught fire, scorching the two men in front of her. With lightning quickness, her hand smacked the desktop, the slap echoing across the room.

"I cannot believe the narrow-minded, right-wing approach of our city's so-called leaders," she snapped, more to herself than to the two in front of her. Then she narrowed on Burridge again. "And is that what you're going to tell McCauley, the media, and the general public — that this department does not believe in promoting people who happen to be homosexual? And they will want to know, because in case you've forgotten, Miranda is a hero. Next month she'll be in Ottawa getting the Governor General's Medal of

Bravery. And the national media will eat this right up. They'll say she's good enough to be a hero, but not good enough to be a bloody sergeant!"

Jane told herself she shouldn't be surprised by Burridge's actions. People like him were part of the reason she never came back to Hooperstown after graduating from the university — they were still stuck in the fifties. And part of the anger and disappointment were reserved for herself, because she had wimped out, fled for the bright lights of the big city, like most other intelligent, ambitious people of her generation.

"Well," Burridge huffed, "we don't have to tell anyone why we're not promoting her, of course."

Jane bristled as she stepped closer to Burridge and smiled. "Oh, they'll know all right. Because I'm going to tell them. And then this town will probably be hit with the biggest lawsuit it's ever seen."

Burridge coughed, feeling more like he was choking to death. He couldn't believe she'd sacrifice the department and the city to some goddamned liberal cause! Yet he knew she'd do it too. She had all the right strings to pull. He knew about the years she'd spent working as an advisor to the government. And word had it she was a big-deal bitch with the National Action Committee on the Status of Women.

Jane stepped back and leaned against the desk again, her face unclenching.

"I'll tell you what the three of us are going to do. We're going to march back in there and make the recommendation we all agreed on after the interviews. And if the other two board members don't like it, too bad. With the three of us in favor of the motion, it'll be carried."

Burridge and Fairborn glanced at each other, knowing they were defeated.

"And if you two don't hold up your end of the bargain, I will resign from the board. And the first thing I'll do is hold a big press conference."

Waiting with Miranda and Miki now were a newspaper reporter and photographer, a radio reporter, and a television crew. The local media were still hungry for anything on the city's hero, and after Miranda had tipped off the paper, word had obviously spread like wildfire.

Everyone jumped to their feet as the doors swung open. Tape recorders flicked on, cameras wound and focused, and spotlights glared.

"Congratulations, Sergeant McCauley," Jane smiled, her hand outstretched as she reached Miranda. If she was surprised by the presence of reporters, she didn't show it.

Miranda smiled back, Miki right by her side throwing her head back in relief and in surprise.

"How does it feel to be promoted?" asked one of the circling reporters.

"Great," Miranda said into the microphone, blinding lights bathing the three.

"Did the shooting have anything to do with the decision?" another asked Jane.

Jane held her head up, eyes as cool and guarded as concrete. No one would ever have to know the arm-twisting she'd just done to make this moment possible.

"Sergeant McCauley deserves this promotion more

than anyone in this department. She earned it before last week's incident, and she certainly has earned it since."

One of the reporters had literally cornered the chief, a microphone stuck nearly up his nose. His face was perspiring, but he was smiling as he answered the questions.

Miranda shot a look in his direction, a self-satisfying grin on her face.

EPILOGUE

Miranda tucked her blue uniform shirt into her pants and zipped them up. Miki, sitting on the bench behind Miranda, laced her combat boots. Miranda moved off to the dirty mirror and clipped her black tie on, catching the reflection of the silver threading of the sergeant's stripes on her sleeve. She smiled. It was her first day to wear the new stripes.

Miki caught her admiring the new markings and smiled too. She blew the embarrassed Miranda a kiss.

"Christ, what a fucking joke!" It sounded like Jeff Rowe's voice drifting over the adjoining men's locker room. It had originally been one large room for the male officers to change in, but once women were hired, they separated the room with a thin layer of pressboard and a row of lockers.

"Yeah," came another voice, full of derision. "A fucking bull dyke to lead us around by the balls. Just because she happens to be flavor of the month around here, the big hero."

Rowe and the mysterious voice grumbled in frustration.

Still looking in the mirror, Miranda caught the reflection of Miki's reddened, angry face. Clutching the sink, Miranda stared into the drain.

"She might be flavor of the month," came the rising voice of Fred Daigle, a twenty-year man on the force, "but neither of you would have put your balls on the line at that house!"

Miranda looked up into the mirror again, her smile growing into a giggle. Miki laughed too until she was rolling on the floor clutching her sides. Miranda's fingers moved up to the raised threading of the stripes on her left arm. She stroked them, feeling the stiffness, the newness of them, the authority of them. They were hers. Not Rowe's, nor any of the others feeling threatened by it. She more than earned those stripes, and she knew she'd have to keep on earning them, every shift.

Miranda turned and gave Miki a reassuring wink.

"C'mon, let's go get 'em."

A few of the publications of
THE NAIAD PRESS, INC.
P.O. Box 10543 • Tallahassee, Florida 32302
Phone (904) 539-5965
Toll-Free Order Number: 1-800-533-1973
Mail orders welcome. Please include 15% postage.

NORTHERN BLUE by Tracey Richardson. 224 pp. Police recruits Miki & Miranda — passion in the line of fire. ISBN 1-56280-118-X $10.95

LOVE'S HARVEST by Peggy Herring. 176 pp. by the author of *Once More With Feeling.* ISBN 1-56280-117-1 10.95

THE COLOR OF WINTER by Lisa Shapiro. 208 pp. Romantic love beyond your wildest dreams. ISBN 1-56280-116-3 10.95

FAMILY SECRETS by Laura DeHart Young. 208 pp. Enthralling romance and suspense. ISBN 1-56280-119-8 10.95

INLAND PASSAGE by Jane Rule. 288 pp. Tales exploring conventional & unconventional relationships. ISBN 0-930044-56-8 10.95

DOUBLE BLUFF by Claire McNab. 208 pp. 7th Detective Carol Ashton Mystery. ISBN 1-56280-096-5 10.95

BAR GIRLS by Lauran Hoffman. 176 pp. See the movie, read the book! ISBN 1-56280-115-5 10.95

THE FIRST TIME EVER edited by Barbara Grier & Christine Cassidy. 272 pp. Love stories by Naiad Press authors. ISBN 1-56280-086-8 14.95

MISS PETTIBONE AND MISS McGRAW by Brenda Weathers. 208 pp. A charming ghostly love story. ISBN 1-56280-151-1 10.95

CHANGES by Jackie Calhoun. 208 pp. Involved romance and relationships. ISBN 1-56280-083-3 10.95

FAIR PLAY by Rose Beecham. 256 pp. 3rd Amanda Valentine Mystery. ISBN 1-56280-081-7 10.95

PAXTON COURT by Diane Salvatore. 256 pp. Erotic and wickedly funny contemporary tale about the business of learning to live together. ISBN 1-56280-109-0 21.95

PAYBACK by Celia Cohen. 176 pp. A gripping thriller of romance, revenge and betrayal. ISBN 1-56280-084-1 10.95

THE BEACH AFFAIR by Barbara Johnson. 224 pp. Sizzling summer romance/mystery/intrigue. ISBN 1-56280-090-6 10.95

GETTING THERE by Robbi Sommers. 192 pp. Nobody does it like Robbi! ISBN 1-56280-099-X 10.95

FINAL CUT by Lisa Haddock. 208 pp. 2nd Carmen Ramirez
Mystery. ISBN 1-56280-088-4   10.95

FLASHPOINT by Katherine V. Forrest. 256 pp. A Lesbian
blockbuster! ISBN 1-56280-079-5   10.95

CLAIRE OF THE MOON by Nicole Conn. Audio Book —Read
by Marianne Hyatt. ISBN 1-56280-113-9   16.95

FOR LOVE AND FOR LIFE: INTIMATE PORTRAITS OF
LESBIAN COUPLES by Susan Johnson. 224 pp.
ISBN 1-56280-091-4   14.95

DEVOTION by Mindy Kaplan. 192 pp. See the movie — read
the book! ISBN 1-56280-093-0   10.95

SOMEONE TO WATCH by Jaye Maiman. 272 pp. 4th Robin
Miller Mystery. ISBN 1-56280-095-7   10.95

GREENER THAN GRASS by Jennifer Fulton. 208 pp. A young
woman — a stranger in her bed. ISBN 1-56280-092-2   10.95

TRAVELS WITH DIANA HUNTER by Regine Sands. Erotic
lesbian romp. Audio Book (2 cassettes) ISBN 1-56280-107-4   16.95

CABIN FEVER by Carol Schmidt. 256 pp. Sizzling suspense
and passion. ISBN 1-56280-089-1   10.95

THERE WILL BE NO GOODBYES by Laura DeHart Young. 192
pp. Romantic love, strength, and friendship. ISBN 1-56280-103-1   10.95

FAULTLINE by Sheila Ortiz Taylor. 144 pp. Joyous comic
lesbian novel. ISBN 1-56280-108-2   9.95

OPEN HOUSE by Pat Welch. 176 pp. 4th Helen Black Mystery.
ISBN 1-56280-102-3   10.95

ONCE MORE WITH FEELING by Peggy J. Herring. 240 pp.
Lighthearted, loving romantic adventure. ISBN 1-56280-089-2   10.95

FOREVER by Evelyn Kennedy. 224 pp. Passionate romance — love
overcoming all obstacles. ISBN 1-56280-094-9   10.95

WHISPERS by Kris Bruyer. 176 pp. Romantic ghost story
ISBN 1-56280-082-5   10.95

NIGHT SONGS by Penny Mickelbury. 224 pp. 2nd Gianna Maglione
Mystery. ISBN 1-56280-097-3   10.95

GETTING TO THE POINT by Teresa Stores. 256 pp. Classic
southern Lesbian novel. ISBN 1-56280-100-7   10.95

PAINTED MOON by Karin Kallmaker. 224 pp. Delicious
Kallmaker romance. ISBN 1-56280-075-2   10.95

THE MYSTERIOUS NAIAD edited by Katherine V. Forrest &
Barbara Grier. 320 pp. Love stories by Naiad Press authors.
ISBN 1-56280-074-4   14.95

DAUGHTERS OF A CORAL DAWN by Katherine V. Forrest.
240 pp. Tenth Anniversay Edition. ISBN 1-56280-104-X   10.95

BODY GUARD by Claire McNab. 208 pp. 6th Carol Ashton
Mystery. ISBN 1-56280-073-6   10.95

CACTUS LOVE by Lee Lynch. 192 pp. Stories by the beloved
storyteller. ISBN 1-56280-071-X   9.95

SECOND GUESS by Rose Beecham. 216 pp. 2nd Amanda Valentine
Mystery. ISBN 1-56280-069-8   9.95

THE SURE THING by Melissa Hartman. 208 pp. L.A. earthquake
romance. ISBN 1-56280-078-7   9.95

A RAGE OF MAIDENS by Lauren Wright Douglas. 240 pp. 6th Caitlin
Reece Mystery. ISBN 1-56280-068-X   10.95

TRIPLE EXPOSURE by Jackie Calhoun. 224 pp. Romantic drama
involving many characters. ISBN 1-56280-067-1   9.95

UP, UP AND AWAY by Catherine Ennis. 192 pp. Delightful
romance. ISBN 1-56280-065-5   9.95

PERSONAL ADS by Robbi Sommers. 176 pp. Sizzling short
stories. ISBN 1-56280-059-0   9.95

FLASHPOINT by Katherine V. Forrest. 256 pp. Lesbian
blockbuster! ISBN 1-56280-043-4   22.95

CROSSWORDS by Penny Sumner. 256 pp. 2nd Victoria Cross
Mystery. ISBN 1-56280-064-7   9.95

SWEET CHERRY WINE by Carol Schmidt. 224 pp. A novel of
suspense. ISBN 1-56280-063-9   9.95

CERTAIN SMILES by Dorothy Tell. 160 pp. Erotic short stories.
ISBN 1-56280-066-3   9.95

EDITED OUT by Lisa Haddock. 224 pp. 1st Carmen Ramirez
Mystery. ISBN 1-56280-077-9   9.95

WEDNESDAY NIGHTS by Camarin Grae. 288 pp. Sexy
adventure. ISBN 1-56280-060-4   10.95

SMOKEY O by Celia Cohen. 176 pp. Relationships on the
playing field. ISBN 1-56280-057-4   9.95

KATHLEEN O'DONALD by Penny Hayes. 256 pp. Rose and
Kathleen find each other and employment in 1909 NYC.
ISBN 1-56280-070-1   9.95

STAYING HOME by Elisabeth Nonas. 256 pp. Molly and Alix
want a baby . . . or do they? ISBN 1-56280-076-0   10.95

TRUE LOVE by Jennifer Fulton. 240 pp. Six lesbians searching
for love in all the "right" places. ISBN 1-56280-035-3   10.95

GARDENIAS WHERE THERE ARE NONE by Molleen Zanger.
176 pp. Why is Melanie inextricably drawn to the old house?
ISBN 1-56280-056-6   9.95

KEEPING SECRETS by Penny Mickelbury. 208 pp. 1st Gianna
Maglione Mystery. ISBN 1-56280-052-3   9.95

THE ROMANTIC NAIAD edited by Katherine V. Forrest &
Barbara Grier. 336 pp. Love stories by Naiad Press authors.
ISBN 1-56280-054-X   14.95

UNDER MY SKIN by Jaye Maiman. 336 pp. 3rd Robin Miller
Mystery.   ISBN 1-56280-049-3.   10.95

STAY TOONED by Rhonda Dicksion. 144 pp. Cartoons — 1st
collection since *Lesbian Survival Manual.*   ISBN 1-56280-045-0   9.95

CAR POOL by Karin Kallmaker. 272pp. Lesbians on wheels
and then some!   ISBN 1-56280-048-5   10.95

NOT TELLING MOTHER: STORIES FROM A LIFE by Diane
Salvatore. 176 pp. Her 3rd novel.   ISBN 1-56280-044-2   9.95

GOBLIN MARKET by Lauren Wright Douglas. 240pp. 5th Caitlin
Reece Mystery.   ISBN 1-56280-047-7   10.95

LONG GOODBYES by Nikki Baker. 256 pp. 3rd Virginia Kelly
Mystery.   ISBN 1-56280-042-6   9.95

FRIENDS AND LOVERS by Jackie Calhoun. 224 pp. Mid-
western Lesbian lives and loves.   ISBN 1-56280-041-8   10.95

THE CAT CAME BACK by Hilary Mullins. 208 pp. Highly
praised Lesbian novel.   ISBN 1-56280-040-X   9.95

BEHIND CLOSED DOORS by Robbi Sommers. 192 pp. Hot,
erotic short stories.   ISBN 1-56280-039-6   9.95

CLAIRE OF THE MOON by Nicole Conn. 192 pp. See the
movie — read the book!   ISBN 1-56280-038-8   10.95

SILENT HEART by Claire McNab. 192 pp. Exotic Lesbian
romance.   ISBN 1-56280-036-1   10.95

HAPPY ENDINGS by Kate Brandt. 272 pp. Intimate conversations
with Lesbian authors.   ISBN 1-56280-050-7   10.95

THE SPY IN QUESTION by Amanda Kyle Williams. 256 pp.
4th Madison McGuire Mystery.   ISBN 1-56280-037-X   9.95

SAVING GRACE by Jennifer Fulton. 240 pp. Adventure and
romantic entanglement.   ISBN 1-56280-051-5   9.95

THE YEAR SEVEN by Molleen Zanger. 208 pp. Women surviving
in a new world.   ISBN 1-56280-034-5   9.95

CURIOUS WINE by Katherine V. Forrest. 176 pp. Tenth Anniver-
sary Edition. The most popular contemporary Lesbian love story.
ISBN 1-56280-053-1   10.95
Audio Book (2 cassettes)   ISBN 1-56280-105-8   16.95

CHAUTAUQUA by Catherine Ennis. 192 pp. Exciting, romantic
adventure.   ISBN 1-56280-032-9   9.95

A PROPER BURIAL by Pat Welch. 192 pp. 3rd Helen Black
Mystery.   ISBN 1-56280-033-7   9.95

SILVERLAKE HEAT: A Novel of Suspense by Carol Schmidt.
240 pp. Rhonda is as hot as Laney's dreams. ISBN 1-56280-031-0   9.95

LOVE, ZENA BETH by Diane Salvatore. 224 pp. The most talked
about lesbian novel of the nineties!   ISBN 1-56280-030-2   10.95

A DOORYARD FULL OF FLOWERS by Isabel Miller. 160 pp.
Stories incl. 2 sequels to *Patience and Sarah.* ISBN 1-56280-029-9   9.95

MURDER BY TRADITION by Katherine V. Forrest. 288 pp. 4th
Kate Delafield Mystery.   ISBN 1-56280-002-7   10.95

THE EROTIC NAIAD edited by Katherine V. Forrest & Barbara
Grier. 224 pp. Love stories by Naiad Press authors.
                                      ISBN 1-56280-026-4   14.95

DEAD CERTAIN by Claire McNab. 224 pp. 5th Carol Ashton
Mystery.   ISBN 1-56280-027-2   9.95

CRAZY FOR LOVING by Jaye Maiman. 320 pp. 2nd Robin Miller
Mystery.   ISBN 1-56280-025-6   9.95

STONEHURST by Barbara Johnson. 176 pp. Passionate regency
romance.   ISBN 1-56280-024-8   10.95

INTRODUCING AMANDA VALENTINE by Rose Beecham.
256 pp. 1st Amanda Valentine Mystery.   ISBN 1-56280-021-3   9.95

UNCERTAIN COMPANIONS by Robbi Sommers. 204 pp.
Steamy, erotic novel.   ISBN 1-56280-017-5   9.95

A TIGER'S HEART by Lauren W. Douglas. 240 pp. 4th Caitlin
Reece Mystery.   ISBN 1-56280-018-3   9.95

PAPERBACK ROMANCE by Karin Kallmaker. 256 pp. A
delicious romance.   ISBN 1-56280-019-1   9.95

MORTON RIVER VALLEY by Lee Lynch. 304 pp. Lee Lynch
at her best!   ISBN 1-56280-016-7   9.95

THE LAVENDER HOUSE MURDER by Nikki Baker. 224 pp.
2nd Virginia Kelly Mystery.   ISBN 1-56280-012-4   9.95

PASSION BAY by Jennifer Fulton. 224 pp. Passionate romance,
virgin beaches, tropical skies.   ISBN 1-56280-028-0   10.95

STICKS AND STONES by Jackie Calhoun. 208 pp. Contemporary
lesbian lives and loves.   ISBN 1-56280-020-5   9.95
Audio Book (2 cassettes)   ISBN 1-56280-106-6   16.95

DELIA IRONFOOT by Jeane Harris. 192 pp. Adventure for Delia
and Beth in the Utah mountains.   ISBN 1-56280-014-0   9.95

UNDER THE SOUTHERN CROSS by Claire McNab. 192 pp.
Romantic nights Down Under.   ISBN 1-56280-011-6   9.95

GRASSY FLATS by Penny Hayes. 256 pp. Lesbian romance in
the '30s.   ISBN 1-56280-010-8   9.95

A SINGULAR SPY by Amanda K. Williams. 192 pp. 3rd
Madison McGuire Mystery.   ISBN 1-56280-008-6   8.95

THE END OF APRIL by Penny Sumner. 240 pp. 1st Victoria
Cross Mystery.   ISBN 1-56280-007-8   8.95

HOUSTON TOWN by Deborah Powell. 208 pp. A Hollis
Carpenter Mystery.   ISBN 1-56280-006-X   8.95

KISS AND TELL by Robbi Sommers. 192 pp. Scorching stories
by the author of *Pleasures.*   ISBN 1-56280-005-1   10.95

STILL WATERS by Pat Welch. 208 pp. 2nd Helen Black Mystery.
                                           ISBN 0-941483-97-5   9.95

TO LOVE AGAIN by Evelyn Kennedy. 208 pp. Wildly romantic
love story.   ISBN 0-941483-85-1   9.95

IN THE GAME by Nikki Baker. 192 pp. 1st Virginia Kelly
Mystery.   ISBN 1-56280-004-3   9.95

AVALON by Mary Jane Jones. 256 pp. A Lesbian Arthurian
romance.   ISBN 0-941483-96-7   9.95

STRANDED by Camarin Grae. 320 pp. Entertaining, riveting
adventure.   ISBN 0-941483-99-1   9.95

THE DAUGHTERS OF ARTEMIS by Lauren Wright Douglas.
240 pp. 3rd Caitlin Reece Mystery.   ISBN 0-941483-95-9   9.95

CLEARWATER by Catherine Ennis. 176 pp. Romantic secrets
of a small Louisiana town.   ISBN 0-941483-65-7   8.95

THE HALLELUJAH MURDERS by Dorothy Tell. 176 pp. 2nd
Poppy Dillworth Mystery.   ISBN 0-941483-88-6   8.95

SECOND CHANCE by Jackie Calhoun. 256 pp. Contemporary
Lesbian lives and loves.   ISBN 0-941483-93-2   9.95

BENEDICTION by Diane Salvatore. 272 pp. Striking, contemporary romantic novel.   ISBN 0-941483-90-8   9.95

BLACK IRIS by Jeane Harris. 192 pp. Caroline's hidden past . . .
                                           ISBN 0-941483-68-1   8.95

TOUCHWOOD by Karin Kallmaker. 240 pp. Loving, May/
December romance.   ISBN 0-941483-76-2   9.95

COP OUT by Claire McNab. 208 pp. 4th Carol Ashton Mystery.
                                           ISBN 0-941483-84-3   9.95

THE BEVERLY MALIBU by Katherine V. Forrest. 288 pp. 3rd
Kate Delafield Mystery.   ISBN 0-941483-48-7   10.95

These are just a few of the many Naiad Press titles — we are the oldest and
largest lesbian/feminist publishing company in the world. Please request a
complete catalog. We offer personal service; we encourage and welcome
direct mail orders from individuals who have limited access to bookstores
carrying our publications.